Only the barest biographical facts about François Villon are available to us; yet these facts—derived primarily from police records and from the internal evidence of his poems—have served as the basis for rich romantic legend. Born in Paris in 1431, his given name either François de Montcorbier or François de Loges, he took the name Villon from the guardian who raised him and provided for his early education. A student at the University of Paris, he obtained his Bachelor of Arts degree in 1449, and his Master of Arts in 1452. In 14[illegible] he was forced to flee Paris for his [illegible]

The Poems of
FRANÇOIS VILLON

A New Translation with an
Introduction by

GALWAY KINNELL

A SIGNET CLASSIC

PUBLISHED BY THE NEW AMERICAN LIBRARY

To
Berta Dominguez D.

Qui ne tenez d'empereur ne de roy
Mais seulement de Dieu de Paradis

First Printing, April, 1965

SIGNET TRADEMARK REG. U.S. PAT. OFF. AND FOREIGN COUNTRIES
REGISTERED TRADEMARK—MARCA REGISTRADA
HECHO EN CHICAGO, U.S.A.

SIGNET CLASSICS *are published by*
The New American Library of World Literature, Inc.
501 Madison Avenue, New York, New York 10022

PRINTED IN THE UNITED STATES OF AMERICA

CONTENTS

Introduction 7

A Note on the Translation 19

A Note on the Text 21

Acknowledgments 22

Le Lais / The Legacy 23

Le Testament / The Testament 45

Poésies Diverses / Miscellaneous Poems 173

Notes

- THE LEGACY 212
- THE TESTAMENT 214
- MISCELLANEOUS POEMS 219

Chronology 220

Selected Bibliography 221

Index of First Lines 223

INTRODUCTION

I

François Villon's life has become a legend, but except for a few anthology pieces his poetry remains little known. The traditional account depicts him as the vagabond poet who dashed off verses—poignant *ballades* and rowdy drinking songs—between bouts of drinking, whoring, thieving, pimping, murdering, and general hell-raising. In the more modern version he is the prototype of the *poète maudit,* spiritual father to Poe, Baudelaire, and Rimbaud. Either way, he himself is exalted and his poetry is ignored. Perhaps a certain contempt for poetry is behind a preoccupation with a poet's life. Anyway, the propagators of the Villon legend do not have anything interesting to say about the poems. By way of criticism they drape the more "romantic" poems in sentimental platitudes, touch upon the ribald character of others, and dismiss the rest—the bulk of Villon's poetry—as hastily thrown together, topical ramblings.

Even the most serious Villon criticism has a strong biographical slant. Villon scholars do not admit that he could have been capable of invention, or could have embroidered on the facts. They examine his poems almost as if they were old letters and diaries. Villon criticism sheds little light on the poems because it doesn't talk about them as poems at all.

At the same time, the legend of Villon's life, which

has so eclipsed the poems, has only a shaky foundation. As the reader can see by looking at the Longnon-Foulet "Sources de notre connaissance de la vie de Villon et de son milieu," [1] we know nearly nothing of the life of this poet. The facts we do know are of an extraordinary kind; the trouble is that we know just enough of these to whet the imagination and just too few to keep it grounded in reality. And while Villon speaks of himself constantly in his poems, his statements can hardly be taken at face value. Like most legends, this one has been built of conjecture, along lines laid down by a cliché. It is well to admit the fabrication if we are to see Villon's poems in their own light.

The moment we look at them as poems, however, we see them defaced by time. We have to ask ourselves if we are in a position to grasp these poems at all. Some scholars believe that the key to this poetry disappeared with Villon and his age, that we can't understand the poems since we know so little of the persons and events they are about. This theory was first put forward in 1533, less than a hundred years after the poems were written, by Clément Marot, Villon's first editor.

> As for the artistry of the bequests that Villon made in his testaments, to understand it truly one would have had to have lived in the Paris of his day and to have known the places, events, and men he speaks about: the more the memory of which fades the less the skill of these bequests will be understood. For this reason whoever wishes to create a poem which will endure will not take as his subject-matter such vulgar and particular matters.

If time had already begun to wear the poetry away, at a period when it was still possible, as Marot says, to find old men who could recite it by heart, how much more inaccessible must it be today?

[1] *François Villon, Oeuvres,* pp. iii-vii.

Help came from an unexpected quarter. Toward the end of the last century a wave of historical research into Villon took place. Spectacularly successful, it turned up references to most of the persons he mentions. For the first time since Villon's day it became possible to identify nearly every character in the poems. The expectation was that these discoveries would illuminate the poems. Sometimes they did, particularly in the cases of antiphrasis. But now that the excitement has faded, we see they did not greatly enlarge our understanding after all. As anyone using a fully annotated edition of Villon finds out, the historical information may tell us a lot about a character's actual life, but as for his function in the poem it nearly always leaves us in the dark. I suspect that the real value of this research will be in teaching us that the past does not hold the key to Villon. It will oblige us to assume that Villon's characters function like the characters in any work of fiction, with the context supplying what we need to know about them. It will oblige us to look at the poems as poems.

Traditional criticism has not done this. It explained a "difficult" passage by citing a historical reference, or maintained that the absence of a historical reference made the passage inexplicable, or dismissed the matter on the grounds that Villon must have been muddled. Old-style critics put on a very condescending air indeed, and why not, if Villon was nothing more than a thief, pimp, and vagabond?

A new kind of criticism is coming into being which admits its ignorance and makes this act of respect for Villon its starting-point. It treats the poems neither as autobiography nor as documents of history but as self-contained works of art. I have in mind two studies, G. A. Brunelli's *François Villon,* particularly the section, "Villon e i Testamenti," which discusses the mock rituals that appear in *The Testament;* and a work in progress, parts of which I have read in manuscript, David Kuhn's *Paradis peint,* a book which starts out with a study of fifteenth-century erotic jargon and goes on, through a discussion of sexual second meanings, to raise the questions, "What are these poems about? What is their intent as poems?" Since he is the first to ask, Mr. Kuhn has to deal with these questions from scratch. The kind of answers he develops opens a whole new way of understanding Villon's poetry. I think the publication of *Paradis peint* will be one of the milestones in Villon studies.

The remarks which follow—in which I try to suggest a way of seeing *The Testament* as a unified and intelligible poem, rather than as a rambling series of private jokes relieved by a few lyrical moments—owe much to the approach of these two critics, especially David Kuhn. I realize, of course, that either man might be surprised, and very possibly dismayed, by the acknowledgment.

II

The literary prototype of both *The Legacy* and *The Testament,* Villon's two major works, is the mock testament, a fairly widespread medieval form which is exemplified by the *testamentum porcelli* and the *testamentum asini (The Pig's Testament* and *The Ass's Testament).*[2] In these works an animal gives away the parts of his body in bequests which are often obscene and which sometimes involve ecclesiastical satire. The pig, for instance, may leave his bones to the dicemaker, his feet to the errand runner, and his sexual part to the priest.

Villon's *Testament* adheres closely to the legal form. It begins with the statement of the testator's age and mental competence and declares that this document represents his last will. It gives the date. It declares that this document supersedes all previous ones. It lists the

[2] An account of these two works as well as of other mock testaments of the Middle Ages can be found in W. H. Rice, *The European Ancestry of Villon's Satirical Testaments.* New York, 1941.

bequests in the proper order: to the Virgin Mary, the Earth, the testator's parents and girl friend; to friends and acquaintances; and to institutions, hospitals, and charities. Toward the end it names an interpreter for the will, specifies the burial place, provides the epitaph, and appoints bell-ringers, executors, probator, and pallbearers.

Among medieval examples of the genre, Villon's satirical *Testament* stands in a class by itself. This is partly because *The Testament* (and *The Legacy* too) is richer in detail, funnier, crueler, livelier, and far more personal than the others. But it is mainly because Villon has taken a form designed for comic purposes and turned it to a new, deeply serious, almost tragic use.

Since both Villon's major poems are examples of the same genre, we can perhaps get some idea of what is special about *The Testament* by looking at *The Legacy,* written five years earlier. If *The Legacy* and *The Testament* were essentially the same poem, if Villon's only reason for writing *The Testament* was that in the years since he wrote *The Legacy* he had made new friends and new enemies and needed a new vehicle for giving them their due, the two poems might closely resemble each other from start to finish. But they diverge very sharply, as I will try to show.

To some readers *The Legacy* looks like sheer horseplay, while to others it seems, at least in part, a work of considerable romantic sadness. (I suspect readers of the latter kind are only trying to impute worth—*i. e.,* poignant sentiments—to a poem they secretly find rather trivial.) Neither description of this strange poem suits it. It is not a romantic piece, but neither is it just some joke Villon casually dashed off. It *is* a joke, but it is one which grows more complex at every reading.

A striking thing about *The Legacy*—and the only point I want to make here—is its curious conglomeration of styles. The poem has three parts, and each is written in a different style. The opening section, a kind of *congé d'amour* in the tradition of Alain Chartier's *Livre de la belle dame sans merci,* depicts in a high-flown, courtly style the plight of a poet martyred by his cruel mistress. The middle section, a mock giving-away of goods, is written in a rapid-fire, direct style, and suggests that the leave-taking is not only from a lady but also from a way of being, a style of life. The last section is written in a manner that parodies the abstract language of Aristotelian psychology.

Surely Villon put these three styles together deliberately. What is in doubt is whether he did so out of caprice or to establish the poem's meaning. Maybe we can't know, for many of the stylistic allusions and mockeries are impossible for us to catch. We can see why the courtly style is used in the opening and why the plain style is used in the middle. Why the poem ends with a take-off on abstract scholastic discourse is less evident.

The poem began as a leave-taking from love; it is odd that love is not mentioned in the concluding stanzas. To see that the last stanzas do have something to say about love one has to make the kind of sexual substitutions that are necessary throughout Villon's work; only then does one discover the auto-erotic second meaning underneath. At this point, the reason for couching the end of this poem in these sterile solipsisms becomes obvious. While the passage is also a generalized, sneering comment on the "mental masturbation" of the Schools, it is more particularly an obscene joke completing the flight from love, which was the undertaking of the poem. From this prankish ending nothing could be more different than the close of *The Testament.*

III

The Testament, also, has three parts: a beginning of about 800 lines, a middle of about 1000 lines, and an end of about 200 lines. The first part is the most complicated, and since it progresses by means of digressions and asides it is not always easy to follow. It deserves the closest reading, for it contains some of the most beautiful poetry in Villon and it also establishes the sense of the whole poem.

In *The Legacy* Villon had set out to free himself from the prison of love; in this poem he is free already. Behind him, he says, lie years of penniless wandering. In fact, the wisecracking satirist of *The Legacy* has been changed into the passionately serious poet of *The Testament*. Here he describes how pain worked on his understanding, and how it happened that he "wandered" to a vision of the City of God:[3]

> Now it is true that after complaints and tears
> And groans of anguish,
> After sadnesses and sorrows,
> Toil and bitter days on the road,
> Suffering, my sleazy feelings
> About as sharp as a ball of wool
> Opened up more than all Averroës'
> Commentaries on Aristotle.
>
> Yet in the depths of my woe
> Wandering without heads or tails
> God, who comforted the Emmaus
> Pilgrims, as the Gospel tells,
> Showed me a fair city
> Blessed with the gift of hope,
> Even the most wretched of sinners,
> God only hates his perseverance.

This deep change toward the serious is apparent in what could be called Villon's "mutability cantos"—which also occur in this opening section—over two hundred lines of poetry on death. In *The Legacy*

[3] I have adopted David Kuhn's reading of this passage as the most satisfactory from all points of view. The "city" traditionally is identified as Moulins, the seat of the Duke of Bourbon, on the ground that *"Esperance"* was the motto of the Bourbons.

"death" was simply a metaphor. Here it is the thing itself, and few poets have evoked it with such astonishing reality and with so little attempt to mask it or compensate for it.

The conventional *ubi sunt* theme, which is the starting point of these "cantos," is soon left behind, and nothing conventional remains by the time they finish. The poems begin among the beautiful, the famous, and the mighty, and end among ordinary persons; they begin in fable and the distant past, and end in actual streets. They neither assert there is peace in heaven nor moralize on the vanity of life on earth. Villon writes in a passion for reality and in deep anguish at its going. Sentiments, in the usual sense, are not involved. He does not find a Grecian urn on which to retain some vanished scene. It has gone, and if he loved it he weeps for it. What he retains, it seems, is only a strange vitality, the vitality of decay, perhaps, or of sorrow, or just of speech. The poems start out by mourning conventionally at the passing of human glory, but all of a sudden we are made to realize that this glory is, as much as it is anything, the laughter and sparkle of an ordinary man or woman. The lament reaches deep into nature, it is a cry not only over the brevity of existence and the coming on of death, but also over this dying life, this life so horrified by death and so deeply in need of it. As I describe these death poems, perhaps I make them sound terribly solemn; in fact they are lighthearted in an odd way, and full of humor.

Directly thereafter, as a corollary, come the stanzas in which Villon renounces love. In this connection, and for the first time, he states that he is dying:

> I feel my thirst coming on,
> I spit white as cotton . . .

The approach of death is a spoof, a pretense called for by the literary form. That Villon intends it as such is made clear later when he summons to his bedside his imaginary secretary to take dictation of the will, which of course is this poem itself. But the taste of the death poems being still in the reader's mouth, it is hard not to have a sense that under the joke this reference to the approach of death is also meant literally, though in feeling this we are perhaps allowing ourselves to be affected more by the Villon legend than by the poem. In any case, once again death seems to be the conventional metaphor of the loss of love. It is not accidental that the only true love poem in *The Testament* is composed to be spoken by another.

This opening section lays the groundwork for the moral satire, which is to become a strong element in the poem. Perhaps it seems that Villon is poorly placed, in point of view of morals, to attack others for their sins. But if a sign that Jesus was the most nearly perfect of men was his tolerance of other men's weaknesses, his refusal to be holier-than-thou, it is one of his lessons that moral satire is an ambiguous undertaking for anyone claiming to be morally good. The only attack wholly untainted by self-righteousness is that of the anti-Christ, the one who has renounced virtue absolutely. In this passage (the last two lines are quoted from Pontius Pilate), that is exactly the role in which Villon casts himself:

> I am not a judge or deputy
> For punishing or pardoning wrongs:
> I am the most imperfect of all,
> Praised be the mild Jesus Christ,
> Through me may they be satisfied,
> What I have written is written.

As the "most imperfect," he is in a position to show that others, who claim to be holy, are just as imperfect, and often more so. In this way, he constructs, on the moral level, a role similar to Socrates' on the intellectual. The point of the Diomedes parable, told so early in *The Testament,* is precisely to establish this role.

The other dominant element in the poem is its sexuality. Kuhn's study of the erotic jargon of Villon's time suggests strongly that the bequests, whatever their surface meanings, at a second level are sexual, consisting mostly of sexual parts, bedmates, and erotic powers —penises, testicles, vaginas, girl friends, lovers, aphrodisiacs, and potency, to name a few—in a symbolism not very far from Freud's. These sexual objects Villon gives away out of the excess of his own sexuality, as if giving life to the dead.

But it is Villon himself, not the recipients, who writes a last testament, who dies. In giving away these sexual bequests he gives away his sexual power, which is his life. He is "love's martyr," and his martyrdom this time means more than being spurned by a mistress. The words "testament" and "testicle," Villon must have known as he titled his poem, come from the same root.

One of the last bequests in *The Testament* is addressed to the *amans enfermes,* the sick-with-love, to whom Alain Chartier, a poet a generation older than Villon, had willed the power to "compose songs, speeches, and poems," so that they might win the hearts of their beloveds and be cured. To this gift Villon adds another:

> *Item,* I give to the sick-with-love
> Besides Alain Chartier's legacy
> At their bedsides, with weeping and tears
> Quickly filled, a holy-water basin
> And a little sprig of eglantine
> Forever green as an aspergillum. . . .

This pagan exorcism ritual, which Christianity absorbed, Villon appropriates in turn. The water to be sprinkled is love's tears, the branch to sprinkle it is the eglantine, the flower of poetry. This ritual healing is perhaps the true undertaking of the poem. In an obscure, half-glimpsed way, the subject of *The Testament,* as of many great works, is the destruction of life and its renewal through art.

I don't mean to deal in arcane significances. It is only

that there are many more avenues into Villon's poetry than have been taken. As for my intention to say something about the unity of *The Testament,* I could say: The beginning sets forth the poet's plight, the middle enacts his ordeal, and the end returns him to reality.

The last section of *The Testament* consists of the funeral preparations and the two final *ballades.* In this section, more than in the other two, *The Testament* stands apart from *The Legacy.* For the first and only time in his poetry, Villon's voice assumes a certain tranquillity. I do not mean it becomes elevated or tragic: the poetry is still full of ironies, jokes, sexual puns, insults, and so on. But things have turned to themselves again, and as if inevitably, due to the force of the meaning, his voice takes on an authority and calmness. The poem has been a long ordeal, and it has been survived.

In the dyptich on which *The Testament* closes, the two great strands of the poem, social satire and sexuality, reappear side by side. The first *ballade* purports to make peace with society, the second to say farewell to sexual love, but in both poems the intent undergoes a reversal. The first *ballade* starts out as if it will go down the list of all the human types and ask forgiveness of each in turn. As long as it addresses only actors, card-sharps, clowns, and the like, it does this gracefully. But the moment it begins addressing the respectable elements, this poem intending to make peace with society suddenly erupts into an attack that is more savage than ever.

The other *ballade,* a farewell to love, becomes virtually a hymn in praise of love—or, anyway, of the pain of love. This is one of poetry's amazing acts of transcendence and transformation, like the celebration of the mudbanks in the culminating pages of *Walden,* for already in *The Testament* are indications that in Villon's case the pain of love consists, at a minimum, of disease and impotence. The beauty, even the sense of a certain blessedness, which pervades this last *ballade,* in which the "spur of love" stabs the poet once more as he dies, is not dispelled by the realization that the spur is not only sexual desire but perhaps also venereal disease. For there is nothing "poetic" anywhere in Villon. His poetry starts from the grossest base, it is made of pain and laughter, and it is indestructible.

The theme of martyrdom with which *The Legacy* began is the theme, we see, on which *The Testament* closes. The earlier poem makes fun of the fancy way of conceiving of the predicament, and *The Testament* transforms those creaking conventions into a new and stunning reality. *The Testament* is the more serious poem, the more lighthearted, and it surpasses the need for mockery of styles, concealment, or horseplay. It has no secrets left, and for this reason, as one gets to know the poem, it grows so truly mysterious.

A NOTE ON THE TRANSLATION

Every translator has the right, at the outset of his volume, to put his failure in the best light. In my case I have tried to make a translation that is faithful to the original and that is alive, and my excuse is that this is not easy to do. Many obscurities still remain in Villon; in the case of passages where I was at a loss I could do no more than provide a word-by-word rendering. Until a perceptive, detailed commentary appears, the reader of Villon has to be ready to find himself now and again completely in the dark.

As for the tone: ever since the nineteenth-century translations, a kind of romantic perfume has clung to the English versions of Villon. I have tried to resist the literary pressure to play the famous lines and images for all their emotional effect. Rather I have tried to keep the poetry factual, harsh and active, hoping thus to find a tone of voice which might better suit the great original.

I decided against using rhyme and meter. When one is writing a poem, the sound and meaning of a word are one inseparable thing, but when one is translating a poem, they become two things, and to keep the rhyme the translator has to adulterate the meaning. What is more expressive of a poet than his images? Yet in rhyming translations we can't ever be sure the images are the poet's. In this translation the reader can at least know that what he is reading closely translates my understanding of what Villon wrote. I have not wittingly padded or cut, repaired or improved the original. And I wonder, do rhyme and meter mean for us what they meant for Villon? It may be that in our day these formal devices have become a dead hand, which it is just as well not to lay on any poetry.

A NOTE ON THE TEXT

The French text used here is based on the Longnon-Foulet text of 1932; it includes many of the readings proposed by André Burger in his *Lexique de la langue de Villon* and retains a few used in Ferdinand Neri's edition of 1923. I have cut down very much on the punctuation used in the modern editions, in hopes of restoring some of the fluidity and ambiguity present in the fifteenth-century manuscripts, which have almost no punctuation beyond a period at the end of each stanza. The titles of the *ballades* have been omitted, as they are the inventions of later editors, and the *rondeau* "Janin l'Avenu" has been dropped, on the ground that Villon probably didn't write it.[1] The poems in jargon have not been included either, for despite much interesting research these poems continue to be more or less unintelligible.

[1] See A. Jeanroy and E. Droz, *Deux MSS de François Villon* (Paris, 1932), pp. xiv-xv.

ACKNOWLEDGMENTS

For throwing light on several obscure passages in the French text, my thanks are due Professor Brian Woledge of University College, London, and Professor Lawton P. G. Peckham of Columbia University. I am grateful as well to a number of friends for reading the English version and making suggestions. My deepest debt, acknowledged in part in the Introduction, is to David Kuhn. His studies of Villon and his sense of the richness of Villon's meanings have opened this poetry for me and have made it possible for me to attempt a serious translation. The suggestions he made in the English version pulled the poetry together time after time; if there are good touches in this translation they are likely his.

LE LAIS

THE LEGACY

LE LAIS

L'an quatre cens cinquante six
Je Françoys Villon escollier
Considerant, de sens rassis,
Le frain aux dens, franc au collier,
Qu'on doit ses œuvres conseillier
Comme Vegece le raconte,
Sage Rommain, grant conseillier,
Ou autrement on se mesconte.

En ce temps que j'ay dit devant
Sur le Noel, morte saison,
Que les loups se vivent du vent
Et qu'on se tient en sa maison
Pour le frimas, pres du tison,
Me vint ung vouloir de brisier
La tres amoureuse prison
Qui souloit mon cuer debrisier.

Je le feis en telle façon,
Voyant celle devant mes yeulx
Consentant a ma desfaçon
Sans ce que ja luy en fust mieulx,
Dont je me dueil et plains aux cieulx
En requerant d'elle venjance
A tous les dieux venerieux
Et du grief d'amours allejance.

Et se j'ay prins en ma faveur
Ces doulx regars et beaux semblans
De tres decevante saveur
Me trespersans jusques aux flans,
Bien ilz ont vers moy les piez blans
Et me faillent au grant besoing,
Planter me fault autres complans
Et frapper en ung autre coing.

THE LEGACY

In the year fourteen fifty-six
I the scholar François Villon
Whereas, being sound of mind,
In harness, champing at the bit, *4*
A man must reflect on his works
As Vegetius advises it,
Wise Roman, great counselor,
Or else he miscalculates. *8*

At the time I said above
Near Christmas, the dead of the year,
When the wolves live on the wind
And men stick to their houses *12*
Against the frost, close by the blaze,
The desire came to me to break
Out of the dungeon of great love
That was wont to break my heart. *16*

I did it in this fashion,
Envisaging her before my eyes
Consenting to my destruction
Without being any happier, *20*
Wherefore I weep and cry to heaven
And sue for revenge upon her
Of all the gods of love
And for relief from love's pain. *24*

And if I took in my favor
Those soft looks and come-ons
Of a very deceitful flavor
Transpiercing me right to the thighs, *28*
They really show me their heels
And fail me in my urgent need,
I have to find fresh fields to plow
And another die to stamp in. *32*

Le regart de celle m'a prins
Qui m'a esté felonne et dure,
Sans ce qu'en riens aye mesprins
Veult et ordonne que j'endure
La mort et que plus je ne dure,
Si n'y voy secours que fouïr,
Rompre veult la vive souldure
Sans mes piteux regretz oïr.

Pour obvier a ces dangiers
Mon mieulx est ce croy de fouïr,
Adieu, je m'en vois a Angiers
Puis qu'el ne me veult impartir
Sa grace ne la me departir,
Par elle meurs les membres sains,
Au fort je suis amant martir
Du nombre des amoureux sains.

Combien que le depart me soit
Dur, si faut il que je l'eslongne,
Comme mon povre sens conçoit
Autre que moy est en quelongne,
Dont oncques soret de Boulongne
Ne fut plus alteré d'umeur,
C'est pour moy piteuse besongne,
Dieu en vueille oïr ma clameur.

Et puis que departir me fault
Et du retour ne suis certain,
Je ne suis homme sans desfault
Ne qu'autre d'acier ne d'estain,
Vivre aux humains est incertain
Et après mort n'y a relaiz,
Je m'en vois en pays loingtain,
Si establis ce present laiz.

I was captured by the gaze of her
Who has been false and cruel to me,
Although I never did her harm
She wills and commands that I suffer *36*
Death and that I cease to be,
I see no way out but flight,
She wants to cut the living tie
Ignoring my most piteous complaints. *40*

To get around these dangers
I think it's best that I go,
Good-bye, I'm on my way to Angers
Since she doesn't choose to bestow *44*
Her favors, even a little part,
In perfect health I die for her,
In fact I'm a martyred lover
Numbered among the saints of love. *48*

Painful as this taking-leave
Will be, I must put her from me,
As my poor wits conceive,
Someone else winds on her spindle, *52*
For which no Boulogne kipper
Was dried or soured worse than me,
For me it's a piteous piece of work,
May God deign to hear my cry. *56*

And since I have to go
And can't be sure of my return,
I'm not a man without flaws
No more than another made of steel or tin, *60*
Life among men is uncertain
And there's no way station after you die,
I go into a far country,
So I draw up this present legacy. *64*

Premierement, ou nom du Pere,
Du Filz et du Saint Esperit
Et de sa glorieuse Mere
Par qui grace riens ne perit,
Je laisse, de par Dieu, mon bruit
A maistre Guillaume Villon
Qui en l'onneur de son nom bruit,
Mes tentes et mon pavillon.

Item, a celle que j'ai dit
Qui si durement m'a chassié
Que je suis de joye interdit
Et de tout plaisir dechassié,
Je laisse mon cuer enchassié
Palle, piteux, mort et transy,
Elle m'a ce mal pourchassié
Mais Dieu luy en face mercy.

Item, a maistre Ythier Marchant
Auquel je me sens tres tenu
Laisse mon branc d'acier tranchant
Ou a maistre Jehan le Cornu
Qui est en gaige detenu
Pour ung escot huit solz montant,
Si vueil selon le contenu
Qu'on leur livre, en le rachetant.

Item, je laisse a Saint Amant
Le Cheval Blanc avec *la Mulle*
Et a Blarru mon dyamant
Et *l'Asne Royé* qui reculle,
Et le decret qui articulle
Omnis utriusque sexus
Contre la Carmeliste bulle
Laisse aux curez, pour mettre sus.

Firstly, in the name of the Father
And of the Son and of the Holy Ghost
And of His glorious Mother
By whose grace no one perishes, *68*
I leave, God willing, my fame
To Master Guillaume Villon
Which resounds in honor of his name,
And my tents and my pavilion. *72*

Item, to her whom I spoke of
Who sent me packing so cruelly
That I am banned from joy
And driven from all pleasure, *76*
I leave my heart in a shrine
Pale, pitiful, dead and gone,
She brought me to this sorry state
But may God forgive her for it. *80*

Item, to Master Ythier Marchant
To whom I feel obligated
I leave my cutlass of biting steel
Or else to Master Jean le Cornu *84*
Which is being held in pawn
On a bill coming to eight *sous,*
I order in these instructions
That they get it, on paying what's due. *88*

Item, I leave to Saint Amant
The White Horse to go with *The She-Mule*
And to Blarru my diamond
And *The Striped Ass* which backs down, *92*
And the decree which articulates
Omnis utriusque sexus
Against the bull of the Carmelites
I leave to the priests, to put across. *96*

Et a maistre Robert Valee
Povre clerjot en Parlement
Qui n'entent ne mont ne vallee
J'ordonne principalement
Qu'on luy baille legierement
Mes brayes estans aux *Trumillieres*
Pour coeffer plus honnestement
S'amye Jehanne de Millieres.

Pour ce qu'il est de lieu honneste
Fault qu'il soit mieulx recompensé
Car le Saint Esperit l'admoneste
Obstant ce qu'il est insensé:
Pour ce je me suis pourpensé,
Puis qu'il n'a sens ne qu'une aulmoire,
A recouvrer sur Maupensé
Qu'on lui baille l'Art de Memoire.

Item, pour assigner la vie
Du dessusdit maistre Robert,
Pour Dieu, n'y ayez point d'envie,
Mes parens vendez mon haubert
Et que l'argent, ou la plus part,
Soit emploié dedans ces Pasques
A acheter a ce poupart
Une fenestre emprès Saint Jaques.

Item, laisse et donne en pur don
Mes gans et ma hucque de soye
A mon amy Jacques Cardon,
Le glan aussi d'une saulsoye
Et tous les jours une grasse oye
Et ung chappon de haulte gresse,
Dix muys de vin blanc comme croye
Et deux procès, que trop n'engresse.

And to Master Robert Valée
Poor junior clerk of Parliament
Who doesn't know a mount from a valley
I order first and foremost *100*
That he receive immediately
My trousers now at *Trumillières*
To dress more realistically
His girl friend Jeanne de Millières. *104*

As he comes from a good family
He ought to get something better
For the Holy Ghost makes it a duty
Given the fact he's a nitwit: *108*
Therefore I've thought it through,
As he has less brains than a closet,
On getting it back from Maupensé
Give him the *Art of Memory*. *112*

Item, to insure a livelihood
For the aforesaid Master Robert,
For God's sake don't envy him this,
My relatives sell my hauberk *116*
And let the money, or most of it,
Be used between now and Easter Week
To purchase for little babyface
A storefront near Saint-Jacques. *120*

Item, I give and leave outright
My silk cape and my gloves
To my friend Jacques Cardon,
Also an acorn from a willow grove *124*
And every day a greasy goose
And a particularly fat capon,
Ten casks of wine white as chalk
And two lawsuits, to keep his weight down. *128*

Item, je laisse a noble homme
Regnier de Montigny trois chiens,
Aussi a Jehan Raguier la somme
De cent frans prins sur tous mes biens,
Mais quoy? Je n'y comprens en riens
Ce que je pourray acquerir,
On ne doit trop prendre des siens
Ne son amy trop surquerir.

Item, au seigneur de Grigny
Laisse la garde de Nijon
Et six chiens plus qu'a Montigny,
Vicestre chastel et donjon,
Et a ce malostru chanjon,
Mouton, qui le tient en procès,
Laisse trois coups d'ung escourjon
Et couchier paix et aise es ceps.

Et a maistre Jaques Raguier
Laisse l'Abruvouër Popin,
Paiches, poires seur gras figuier,
Tousjours le chois d'ung bon loppin,
Le trou de *la Pomme de Pin,*
Clos et couvert, au feu la plante,
Emmailloté en jacoppin,
Et qui voudra planter si plante.

Item, a maistre Jehan Mautaint
Et maistre Pierre Basanier
Le gré du seigneur qui attaint
Troubles, forfaiz, sans espargnier,
Et a mon procureur Fournier
Bonnetz cours, chausses semelees
Taillees sur mon cordouannier
Pour porter durant ces gelees.

Item, I leave to nobleman
Regnier de Montigny three dogs,
Also to Jean Raguier the sum
Of a hundred *francs* raised on all my goods, *132*
But wait, naturally I'm not including
Anything I still stand to gain,
One shouldn't sponge too much on kin
Or borrow too much from a friend. *136*

Item, to the lord of Grigny
I give the watchtower of Nijon
And six dogs more than to Montigny
And Bicêtre the castle and dungeon, *140*
And to that aborted creep,
Mouton, who ties him up in court,
I leave three strokes of the whip
And a nice quiet sleep in irons. *144*

And to Master Jacques Raguier
I leave the Popin waterhole,
Peaches and pears from the fat figtree,
The standing choice of a nice morsel *148*
And the dive *The Pine Cone,*
Cosy and warm, feet at the blaze,
Swaddled like a Jacobin,
And whom he wants to plow let him plow. *152*

Item, to Master Jean Mautaint
And Master Pierre Basanier
The favor of the lord who arraigns
Brawls and crimes unsparingly, *156*
And to Fournier my lawyer
Short bonnets and hose with soles
Made up at my cobbler's
For snuggling in, these icy spells. *160*

Item, a Jehan Trouvé bouchier
Laisse *le Mouton* franc et tendre
Et ung tacon pour esmouchier
Le Beuf Couronné qu'on veult vendre
Et *la Vache:* qui pourra prendre
Le vilain qui la trousse au col,
S'il ne la rent, qu'on le puist pendre
Et estrangler d'ung bon licol.

Item, au Chevalier du Guet
Le Hëaulme luy establis
Et aux pietons qui vont d'aguet
Tastonnant par ces establis
Je leur laisse ung beaux riblis,
La Lanterne a la Pierre au Let,
Voire, mais j'auray *les Troys Lis*
S'ilz me mainent en Chastellet.

Item, a Perrenet Marchant
Qu'on dit le Bastart de la Barre
Pour ce qu'il est tres bon marchant
Luy laisse trois gluyons de fuerre
Pour estendre dessus la terre
A faire l'amoureux mestier
Ou il luy fauldra sa vie querre
Car il ne scet autre mestier.

Item, au Loup et a Cholet
Je laisse a la fois ung canart
Prins sur les murs comme on souloit
Envers les fossez, sur le tart,
Et a chascun ung grant tabart
De cordelier jusques aux piez,
Busche, charbon et poix au lart
Et mes houseaulx sans avantpiez.

Item, to butcher Jean Trouvé
I leave *The Sheep* gamboling and fresh
And a cat-o'-nine tails to swat
The Crowned Ox which can be bought 164
And *The Cow*: whoever can catch
The guy toting her off on his shoulder,
If he won't give her back, string up
And strangle him with a strong halter. 168

Item, to the Knight of the Watch
I bestow *The Helmet*
And to the flatfoots going on watch
Feeling past these establishments 172
I leave a handsome larceny,
The Lantern on Rue Pierre-au-Lait,
Yes, but I'll have *The Three Lilies*
If they put me in the Châtelet. 176

Item, to Perrenet Marchant
Known as the Bastard of the Bar
Because he's a go-getting merchant
I leave three bundles of straw 180
For spreading on the ground
And there filling amorous orders
By which he'll have to make his living
For it's the only trade he knows. 184

Item, to Loup and to Cholet
I leave one duck between them both
Grabbed off the walls the way we used to
Not far from the moats, late at night, 188
And to each of them the big tabard
Of a Franciscan reaching to the shoes,
Fagots, lump-coal and peas in lard
And my boots without the toe-piece. 192

Item, je laisse en pitié
A trois petis enfans tous nus
Nommez en ce present traictié,
Povres orphelins impourveus
Tous deschaussiez, tous desvestus
Et desnuez comme le ver,
J'ordonne qu'ilz soient pourveus
Au moins pour passer cest yver.

Premierement, Colin Laurens,
Girart Gossouyn et Jehan Marçeau,
Despourveus de biens, de parens,
Qui n'ont vaillant l'ance d'ung seau:
Chascun de mes biens ung fesseau
Ou quatre blans, s'ilz l'ayment mieulx,
Ilz mengeront maint bon morceau,
Les enfans, quant je seray vieulx.

Item, ma nominacion
Que j'ay de l'Université
Laisse par resignacion
Pour seclurre d'aversité
Povres clers de ceste cité
Soubz cest *intendit* contenus,
Charité m'y a incité
Et Nature, les voiant nus.

C'est maistre Guillaume Cotin
Et maistre Thibault de Victry,
Deux povres clers parlans latin,
Paisibles enfans, sans estry,
Humbles, bien chantans au lectry,
Je leur laisse cens recevoir
Sur la maison Guillot Gueuldry
En attendant de mieulx avoir.

Item, I leave out of pity
To three little naked children
Named in this document,
Poor destitute orphans *196*
All unshod and all unclad
And stripped naked as worms,
I order they be provided for
At least to get them through the winter. *200*

First is Colin Laurens,
Then Girard Gossouyn and Jean Marceau,
Who haven't parents or property
Or the price of a bucket-handle: *204*
To each an armload of my goods
Or four *blancs,* as they prefer,
They'll have eaten many a meal,
These kids, by the time I'm old. *208*

Item, my nomination
Got from the University
I bequeath by resignation
To shelter from adversity *212*
Poor clerks of the city
Whose names are cited below,
Charity has put me to it
And Nature, seeing them naked. *216*

They are Master Guillaume Cotin
And Master Thibault de Victry,
Two poor clerks who speak Latin,
Peaceable unsquabbly boys, *220*
Meek, and good at singing with the choir,
I leave them the rent in arrears
On Guillaume Gueuldry's hostel
While waiting for something better. *224*

Item, et j'adjoings a la crosse
Celle de la rue Saint Anthoine
Ou ung billart de quoy on crosse
Et tous les jours plain pot de Saine:
Aux pijons qui sont en l'essoine
Enserrez soubz trappe volliere
Mon mirouër bel et ydoine
Et la grace de la geolliere.

Item, je laisse aux hospitaux
Mes chassiz tissus d'arigniee,
Et aux gisans soubz les estaux
Chascun sur l'œil une grongniee,
Trembler a chiere renfrongniee,
Megres, velus et morfondus,
Chausses courtes, robe rongniee,
Gelez, murdris et enfondus.

Item, je laisse a mon barbier
Les rongneures de mes cheveulx
Plainement et sans destourbier,
Au savetier mes souliers vieulx
Et au freppier mes habitz tieulx
Que quant du tout je les delaisse
Pour moins qu'ilz ne cousterent neufz
Charitablement je leur laisse.

Item, je laisse aux Mendians,
Aux Filles Dieu et aux Beguines
Savoureux morceaulx et frians,
Flaons, chappons, grasses gelines
Et puis preschier les Quinze Signes
Et abatre pain a deux mains,
Carmes chevauchent noz voisines
Mais cela ce n'est que du mains.

Item, to their crooks I add on
The one on the Rue Saint-Antoine
Or a billiard crook for shooting it in
And every day a full glass of Seine: 228
To the pigeons that are in pain
Squeezed in the bird cage
My beautiful, befitting mirror
And an in with the jailer's wife. 232

Item, I leave to the hospitals
My windows woven of spiderwebs,
And to the bums flopped under stalls
A blow in the eye apiece, 236
May they tremble and glower,
Skinny, stubbled, chilled blue,
Pants too short, coats in tatters,
Frozen, beat up and soaked through. 240

Item, I leave to my barber
The old hair from my haircuts
Outright and unconditionally,
My old shoes to the cobbler 244
And to the ragman my old clothes
As they'll be when I'm done with them
For less than what they cost me new
Most charitably I'll let them go. 248

Item, I leave to the Mendicants,
The Daughters of God and the Beguines
Appetizing morsels and tidbits,
Cream-cakes, capons and fat hens 252
And then to preach the Fifteen Signs
And knock down bread with both hands,
Carmelites mount the neighbors' wives
But actually that's the least of it. 256

Item, laisse *le Mortier d'Or*
A Jehan l'espicier de la Garde
Une potence de Saint Mor
Pour faire ung broyer a moustarde:
A celluy qui fist l'avant garde
Pour faire sur moy griefz exploiz
De par moy saint Anthoine l'arde!
Je ne luy feray autre laiz.

Item, je laisse a Merebeuf
Et a Nicolas de Louvieux
A chascun l'escaille d'ung œuf
Plaine de frans et d'escus vieulx:
Quant au concierge de Gouvieulx,
Pierre de Rousseville, ordonne
Pour le donner entendre mieulx
Escus telz que le Prince donne.

Finablement, en escripvant
Ce soir, seulet, estant en bonne,
Dictant ces laiz et descripvant,
J'oïs la cloche de Serbonne
Qui tousjours a neuf heures sonne
Le Salut que l'Ange predit,
Si suspendis et mis en bonne
Pour prier comme le cuer dit.

Ce faisant je m'entroublié
Non pas par force de vin boire
Mon esperit comme lié
Lors je sentis dame Memoire
Reprendre et mettre en son aumoire
Ses especes collateralles,
Oppinative faulce et voire,
Et autres intellectualles.

Item, I leave *The Golden Mortar*
To the spice-seller Jean de la Garde
And also a crutch from Saint-Maur
To use as a pestle for mustard: *260*
To the one who went out of his way
To wreak on me his filthy deeds
For my sake may Saint-Anthony fry him!
I will make him no other legacy. *264*

Item, I leave to Mereboeuf
And Nicolas de Louvieux
An eggshell each
Filled with *francs* and old *écus:* *268*
As for the Gouvieux jailer,
Pierre de Rousseville, I stipulate
So he'll grasp my meaning easier
Ecus of the kind the Prince gives out. *272*

Lastly, as I sat writing
This evening, alone, in good spirits,
Composing and setting down these legacies,
I heard the bell of the Sorbonne *276*
Which always rings at the ninth hour
The Salvation the Angel foretold,
So I stopped and wrote no further
In order to pray as the heart bid. *280*

In doing so I grew muddled
Not from any wine I'd had
But as if my spirit had been shackled
Whereupon I felt Lady Memory *284*
Take up and put in her bureau
Her species collateral,
The opinative both false and true,
And others intellectual. *288*

Et mesmement l'estimative
Par quoy prospective nous vient,
Similative, formative
Desquelles souvent il advient
Que par leur trouble homme devient
Fol et lunatique par mois,
Je l'ay leu se bien m'en souvient
En Aristote aucunes fois.

Dont le sensitif s'esveilla
Et esvertua fantasie
Qui tous organes resveilla
Et tint la souvraine partie
En suspens et comme amortie
Par oppression d'oubliance
Qui en moy s'estoit espartie
Pour monstrer de sens l'aliance.

Puis que mon sens fut a repos
Et l'entendement demeslé
Je cuidé finer mon propos
Mais mon ancre estoit gelé
Et mon cierge trouvé soufflé,
De feu je n'eusse peu finer,
Si m'endormis tout enmouflé
Et ne peus autrement finer.

Fait au temps de ladite date
Par le bien renommé Villon
Qui ne menjue figue ne date,
Sec et noir comme escouvillon
Il n'a tente ne pavillon
Qu'il n'ait laissié a ses amis
Et n'a mais qu'ung peu de billon
Qui sera tantost a fin mis.

And likewise the estimative
Which is what gives us foresight,
The similative, the formative
By which it often comes about *292*
That through their disorder one can go
Mad and lunatic by the month,
I've read this if I remember right
In Aristotle more than once. *296*

At which the sensory awoke
And put fantasy on the alert
Which roused up all the organs
And held the sovereign part *300*
In suspense, as if deadened
By the oppression of forgetfulness
Which spread all through me
Proving the connection of the senses. *304*

As soon as my mind was at rest
And my understanding had cleared
I tried to finish my task
But my ink was frozen *308*
And I saw my candle had blown out,
I couldn't have found any fire,
So I fell asleep all muffled up
And couldn't put on a real ending. *312*

Done on the aforesaid date
By the very renowned Villon
Who doesn't eat, shit, or piss,
Dry and black like a furnace mop *316*
He doesn't have a tent or pavilion
That he hasn't left to a friend,
All he's got is a little change
That will soon come to an end. *320*

[illegible]

[illegible] candle [illegible] blown [illegible]

[illegible]

LE TESTAMENT

THE TESTAMENT

LE TESTAMENT

En l'an de mon trentiesme aage
Que toutes mes hontes j'eus beues,
Ne du tout fol ne du tout sage
Non obstant maintes peines eues
Lesquelles j'ay toutes receues
Soubz la main Thibault d'Aussigny.
S'evesque il est, seignant les rues,
Qu'il soit le mien je le regny.

Mon seigneur n'est ne mon evesque,
Soubz luy ne tiens s'il n'est en friche,
Foy ne luy doy n'hommage avecque,
Je ne suis son serf ne sa biche:
Peu m'a d'une petite miche
Et de froide eaue tout ung esté,
Large ou estroit, moult me fut chiche,
Tel luy soit Dieu qu'il m'a esté.

Et s'aucun me vouloit reprendre
Et dire que je le mauldis
Non fais, se bien le scet comprendre,
En riens de luy je ne mesdis:
Vecy tout le mal que j'en dis,
S'il m'a esté misericors
Jhesus le roy de Paradis
Tel luy soit, a l'ame et au corps.

Et s'esté m'a dur et cruel
Trop plus que cy ne le raconte
Je vueil que le Dieu eternel
Luy soit donc semblable a ce compte,
"Et l'Eglise nous dit et compte
Que prions pour noz ennemis,"
Je vous diray: "J'ay tort et honte,
Quoi qu'il m'ait fait, a Dieu remis."

THE TESTAMENT

In the time of my thirtieth year
When I had drunk down all my shames,
Not all foolish and not all wise
Despite the many blows I had *4*
Every one of which I got
In the clutches of Thibault d'Aussigny,
He may be a bishop, blessing the streets,
But that he is mine I deny. *8*

He isn't my lord or my bishop either,
I hold of him nothing but waste,
I owe him no fealty or homage,
I'm not his serf or little deer: *12*
He fatted me up on a small loaf
And cold water all one summer through,
Generous or tight, to me he was stingy,
May God be to him as he's been to me. *16*

If somebody should want to object
And say that I'm damning the man
I'm not, if you can see the point,
I'm not at all running him down: *20*
Here is the sum of my abuse,
If he showed me any mercy
May Jesus King of Paradise
Show him as much, to soul and body. *24*

If he was cruel and hard to me
Far worse than I tell about here
I ask that the Eternal Lord
Deal likewise with him for this affair, *28*
"But the Church bids and teaches
That we pray for our enemies,"
I'll reply, "I'm wrong and ashamed,
Whatever he did being in God's hands." *32*

Si prieray pour luy de bon cuer
Et pour l'ame de feu Cotart,
Mais quoy? ce sera donc par cuer
Car de lire je suis fetart:
Priere en feray de Picart,
S'il ne le scet voise l'aprendre,
S'il m'en croit, ains qu'il soit plus tart,
A Douai ou a l'Isle en Flandre.

Combien, se oÿr veult qu'on prie
Pour luy, foy que doy mon baptesme,
Obstant qu'a chascun ne le crye
Il ne fauldra pas a son esme:
Ou Psaultier prens quant suis a mesme
Qui n'est de beuf ne cordouen
Le verselet escript septiesme
Du psëaulme *Deus laudem*.

Si prie au benoist fils de Dieu
Qu'a tous mes besoings je reclame,
Que ma povre priere ait lieu
Vers luy de qui tiens corps et ame,
Qui m'a preservé de maint blasme
Et franchy de ville puissance,
Loué soit il et Nostre Dame
Et Loÿs le bon roy de France,

Auquel doint Dieu l'eur de Jacob
Et de Salmon l'onneur et gloire,
Quant de proesse il en a trop,
De force aussi, par m'ame, voire,
En ce monde cy transsitoire
Tant qu'il a de long ne de lé
Affin que de luy soit memoire
Vivre autant que Mathusalé,

Therefore I'll pray for him willingly
And for the soul of the dead Cotart,
But how? It will be by heart
For in matters of reading I'm lazy: *36*
I'll say him a prayer Picard style,
If he doesn't know it let him go learn it,
If he values my advice, before it's too late,
At Douai or at Lille in Flanders. *40*

But if he wants a prayer he can hear,
By the faith I owe from baptism,
Though I won't shout it everywhere
He will not fail to get his wish: *44*
In my psalter when I have the time
Bound neither in hide nor cordovan
I'll recite verse number seven
Of the psalm *Deus laudem.* *48*

So I pray to the blessed Son of God
To whom I turn in all my troubles,
May my poor prayer be admitted
Before Him of whom I hold body and soul, *52*
Who has shielded me from many harms
And delivered me from iron rule,
Praise be to Him and Our Lady
And Louis the good king of France, *56*

To whom may God grant Jacob's luck
And Solomon's honor and glory,
As for prowess he has more than enough
And strength too, by my soul, truly, *60*
In this world that is so fleeting
Such as it has of length and breadth
That the memory of him may remain
May he live as long as Methuselah, *64*

Et douze beaux enfans tous masles,
Vëoir, de son cher sang royal
Aussi preux que fut le grant Charles,
Conceus en ventre nupcial,
Bons comme fut sainct Marcial,
Ainsi en preigne au feu Dauphin,
Je ne luy souhaitte autre mal
Et puis Paradis en la fin.

Pour ce que foible je me sens
Trop plus de biens que de santé
Tant que je suis en mon plain sens,
Si peu que Dieu m'en a presté
Car d'autre ne l'ay emprunté,
J'ay ce testament tres estable
Faict, de derniere voulenté,
Seul pour tout et irrevocable.

Escript l'ay l'an soixante et ung
Lors que le roy me delivra
De la dure prison de Mehun
Et que vie me recouvra,
Dont suis, tant que mon cuer vivra,
Tenu vers luy m'humilier
Ce que feray jusques il moura,
Bienfait ne se doit oublier.

Or est vray qu'après plainz et pleurs
Et angoisseux gemissemens,
Après tristesses et douleurs,
Labeurs et griefz cheminemens,
Travail, mes lubres sentemens
Esguisez comme une pelote
M'ouvrit plus que tous les Commens
D'Averroÿs sur Aristote.

And see twelve fine children all males,
Born of his precious royal stock
As doughty as was the great Charles
Conceived in holy wedlock *68*
And as worthy as Saint Martial,
May it be so for the former Dauphin,
I wish him no other troubles
And Paradise in the end. *72*

Because I'm feeling poor
In goods far more than in health
And as I still have my wits about me,
The few God lent me *76*
For I haven't borrowed from anyone else,
I have drawn up this true and authentic
Testament of my last will,
Once and for all and irrevocable. *80*

Written in the year sixty-one
When the good king delivered me
From the hard prison at Meung
And gave me my life again, *84*
For which I'm bound, while my heart lives,
To humble myself before him
Which I shall do until he dies,
A good deed must not be forgotten. *88*

Now it is true that after complaints and tears
And groans of anguish,
After sadnesses and sorrows,
Toil and bitter days on the road, *92*
Suffering, my sleazy feelings
About as sharp as a ball of wool
Opened up more than all Averroës'
Commentaries on Aristotle. *96*

Combien au plus fort de mes maulx
En cheminant sans croix ne pille
Dieu qui les pelerins d'Esmaus
Conforta, ce dit l'Evangille,
Me monstra une bonne ville
Et pourveue du don d'esperance,
Combien que le pecheur soit ville
Riens ne hayt que perseverance.

Je suis pecheur, je le sçay bien,
Pourtant ne veult pas Dieu ma mort
Mais convertisse et vive en bien
Et tout autre que pechié mort:
Combien qu'en pechié soye mort
Dieu vit et sa misericorde,
Se conscience me remort
Par sa grace pardon m'accorde.

Et comme le noble Rommant
De la Rose dit et confesse
En son premier commencement,
"Qu'on doit jeune cuer en jeunesse,
Quant on le voit viel en viellesse,
Excuser," helas, il dit voir,
Ceulx donc qui me font telle presse
En meurté ne me vouldroient veoir.

Se pour ma mort le bien publique
D'aucune chose vaulsist mieulx
A mourir comme ung homme inique
Je me jujasse, ainsi m'aist Dieux:
Griefz ne faiz a jeunes n'a vieulx
Soie sur piez ou soie en biere,
Les mons ne bougent de leurs lieux
Pour ung povre, n'avant n'arriere.

Yet in the depths of my woe
Wandering without heads or tails
God who comforted the Emmaus
Pilgrims, as the Gospel tells, *100*
Showed me a fair city
Blessed with the gift of hope,
Even the most wretched of sinners,
God only hates his perseverance. *104*

I'm a sinner, I know very well,
And yet God does not wish me to die
But to reform and live in virtue
And all others whom sin bites into: *108*
Although in sin I am dead
God and His mercifulness live,
If in truth my conscience gnaws
He in His grace forgives me. *112*

And as the noble *Roman*
De la Rose states and sets forth
In its very beginning,
"The young heart in its youth, *116*
When seen grown old in its age,
Must be forgiven," alas, it's true,
Which is why those who hound me
Would hate to see me grow old. *120*

If it would help the public weal
In any way for me to die
To be put to death like an evil man
I'd condemn myself, so help me God: *124*
I cause no harm to young or old
Whether upright or in the grave,
Mountains don't budge from their spots
Forward nor back, if you're poor. *128*

Ou temps qu'Alixandre regna
Ung homs nommé Diomedès
Devant luy on luy amena
Engrillonné poulces et des
Comme ung larron, car il fut des
Escumeurs que voions courir,
Si fut mis devant ce cadès
Pour estre jugié a mourir.

L'empereur si l'araisonna,
"Pourquoi es tu larron en mer?"
L' autre responce luy donna,
"Pourquoi larron me faiz clamer?
Pour ce qu'on me voit escumer
En une petiote fuste?
Se comme toy me peusse armer
Comme toy empereur je feusse.

"Mais que veux-tu? De ma fortune
Contre que ne puis bonnement,
Qui si faulcement me fortune,
Me vient tout ce gouvernement:
Excusez moy aucunement
Et saichiez qu'en grant povreté,
Ce mot se dit communement,
Ne gist pas grande loyauté."

Quant l'empereur ot remiré
De Diomedès tout le dit,
"Ta fortune je te mueray
Mauvaise en bonne", si luy dit,
Si fist il: onc puis ne mesdit
A personne mais fut vray homme,
Valere pour vray le baudit
Qui fut nommé le Grant a Romme.

In the time when Alexander reigned
A man by the name of Diomedes
Was brought in before him
His thumbs and fingers in screws *132*
Like a thief, for he was one
Of the pirates we see roving the seas,
Thus he was put before this captain
To receive the death-sentence. *136*

The Emperor took this tack with him,
"Why are you a pirate at sea?"
To which the other answered,
"Why do you call me pirate? *140*
Because I'm seen on the prowl
In a little toy of a galley?
If I could arm myself like you
Like you I'd be an emperor. *144*

"But there it is. From Fortune
Against whose will I'm powerless,
Who cheats me as she deals my fortune,
Comes the course of life I've taken: *148*
Show some understanding
And know that in great poverty,
As the popular saying has it,
There lies no great honesty." *152*

When the Emperor had thought over
Everything Diomedes had said,
"I'll have your fortune changed
From bad to good," he told him, *156*
And so he did: he never maligned
Anyone again but was an honest man,
This is vouched for by Valerian
Who was called "The Great" in Rome. *160*

Se Dieu m'eust donné rencontrer
Ung autre piteux Alixandre
Qui m'eust fait en bon eur entrer
Et lors qui m'eust veu condescendre
A mal, estre ars et mis en cendre
Jugié me feusse de ma voix,
Necessité fait gens mesprendre
Et faim saillir le loup du bois.

Je plains le temps de ma jeunesse
Ouquel j'ay plus qu'autre gallé
Jusques a l'entree de viellesse
Qui son partement m'a celé:
Il ne s'en est a pié allé
N'a cheval, helas, comment don?
Soudainement s'en est vollé
Et ne m'a laissié quelque don.

Allé s'en est et je demeure
Povre de sens et de savoir,
Triste, failly, plus noir que meure,
Qui n'ay ne cens, rente, n'avoir:
Des miens le mendre, je dis voir,
De me desavouer s'avance
Oubliant naturel devoir
Par faulte d'ung peu de chevance.

Si ne crains avoir despendu
Par friander ne par leschier,
Par trop amer n'ay riens vendu
Qu'amis me puissent reprouchier,
Au moins qui leur couste moult chier,
Je le dy et ne croy mesdire,
De ce je me puis revenchier,
Qui n'a mesfait ne le doit dire.

If God had just let me encounter
Some merciful Alexander
Who'd have put me on to good luck
And if I'd then been seen stooping *164*
To evil, to be burnt to ashes
I'd have sentenced myself my own judge,
Necessity makes people err
And hunger beats wolf from wood. *168*

I regret the time of my youth
When more than most I had my fling
Until the entry of old age,
Which kept secret it was leaving: *172*
It did not go away on foot
Or on horseback, alas, how then?
All of a sudden it took flight
And didn't leave me a bone. *176*

It has gone and I stay on
Poor in sense and in knowledge,
Sad, sick, blacker than a mulberry,
Without cents, rent, or goods: *180*
The last of my kin, I swear,
Steps up to disown me
Forgetting the ties of nature
For lack of a bit of money. *184*

No fear I've thrown it away
On good eating or lechery,
Swept away by love I've sold nothing
For which my friends could reproach me, *188*
Anyway nothing that cost them much,
I know I don't lie in saying this,
On this count I can defend myself,
He who hasn't sinned ought not confess. *192*

Bien est verté que j'ay amé
Et ameroie voulentiers
Mais triste cuer, ventre affamé
Qui n'est rassasié au tiers
M'oste des amoureux sentiers,
Au fort, quelqu'ung s'en recompence
Qui est ramply sur les chantiers
Car la dance vient de la pance.

Hé Dieu, se j'eusse estudié
Ou temps de ma jeunesse folle
Et a bonnes meurs dedié
J'eusse maison et couche molle,
Mais quoi? je fuyoie l'escolle
Comme fait le mauvais enfant,
En escripvant ceste parolle
A peu que le cuer ne me fent.

Le dit du Saige trop luy feiz
Favorable (bien en puis mais)
Qui dit, "Esjoÿs toy, mon filz,
En ton adolescence", mais
Ailleurs sert bien d'ung autre mes,
Car, "Jeunesse et adolescence",
C'est son parler ne moins ne mais,
"Ne sont qu'abus et ignorance".

Mes jours s'en sont allez errant
Comme, dit Job, "d'une touaille
Font les filetz quant tisserant
En son poing tient ardente paille",
Lors s'il y a nul bout qui saille
Soudainement il le ravit,
Si ne crains plus que rien m'assaille
Car a la mort tout s'assouvit.

I have loved, it's perfectly true,
And I would again with delight
But a sad heart and starved craw
Hardly satisfied by a third *196*
Pluck me from the paths of love,
Let someone else make up the loss
Who's filled to the brim on the gantry
For the dance is from the belly. *200*

Ah God, if only I'd studied
In the days of my foolish youth
And tried to acquire good habits
I'd have a house and a soft bed, *204*
But what did I do? I ran from that school
Like some good-for-nothing kid,
As I put all this in writing
My heart's on the point of breaking. *208*

I credited the sage's words
Far too much (only I'm to blame)
Who says, "Rejoice, my son,
In the time of your youth," however *212*
He dishes it out differently elsewhere,
When he says, "Childhood and youth,"
These are his words no less no more,
"Are merely ignorance and error." *216*

My days have gone swiftly away,
Just as, says Job, "the threads do
On a cloth, when the weaver
Takes a burning straw in his hand," *220*
Then if an end is sticking out
He razes it in a flash,
So I don't fear whatever's in store
For in death all things are appeased. *224*

Ou sont les gracieux gallans
Que je suivoye ou temps jadis
Si bien chantans, si bien parlans,
Si plaisans en faiz et en dis?
Les aucuns sont morts et roidis,
D'eulx n'est il plus riens maintenant,
Repos aient en paradis
Et Dieu saulve le remenant.

Et les autres sont devenus,
Dieu mercy, grans seigneurs et maistres,
Les autres mendient tous nus
Et pain ne voient qu'aux fenestres,
Les autres sont entrez en cloistres
De Celestins et de Chartreux,
Botez, housez, com pescheurs d'oistres,
Voyez l'estat divers d'entre eux.

Aux grans maistres Dieu doint bien faire
Vivans en paix et en requoy,
En eulx il n'y a que refaire
Si s'en fait bon taire tout quoy,
Mais aux povres qui n'ont de quoy,
Comme moy, Dieu doint patience,
Aux autres ne fault qui ne quoy
Car assez ont pain et pitance.

Bon vins ont, souvent embrochiez,
Saulces, brouetz et gros poissons,
Tartes, flans, oefz fritz et pochiez,
Perdus et en toutes façons:
Pas ne ressemblent les maçons
Que servir fault a si grant peine,
Ilz ne veulent nuls eschançons,
De soy verser chascun se peine.

Where are the happy young men
Whom I followed in the old days
So gifted at singing and talking,
So graceful in word and deed? *228*
Some of them are dead and stiff,
Nothing remains of them any more,
May they find rest in Paradise
And may God save those who are left. *232*

And of these some have become,
Praise God, great lords and masters,
And some half-naked go begging
And see bread only in windows, *236*
And some have entered the cloisters
Of the Celestines and Carthusians,
Booted and gaitered like oyster fishers,
See how differently they've come out. *240*

To the masters may God give good works
While living in peace and quiet,
There's nothing to be done about these
So I'll shut up and keep still, *244*
But to the poor who've nothing at all,
Like me, may God give patience,
To the others—no need this or that
For they've plenty of bread and their pittance. *248*

Good wines they have, constantly broached,
Sauces, broths and fat fishes
Tarts, custards, eggs fried, poached,
Beat up and cooked all kinds of ways: *252*
They aren't a bit like the masons
Who've got to be waited on hand and foot,
These have no use for bottle-yeomen
And each is quick to pour his own. *256*

En cest incident me suis mis
Qui de riens ne sert a mon fait,
Je ne suis juge ne commis
Pour pugnir n'absoudre mesfait,
De tous suis le plus imparfait,
Loué soit le doulx Jhesu Crist,
Que par moy leur soit satisfait,
Ce que j'ay escript est escript.

Laissons le moustier ou il est,
Parlons de chose plus plaisante,
Ceste matiere a tous ne plaist,
Ennuyeuse est et desplaisante:
Povreté, chagrine, dolente,
Tousjours despiteuse et rebelle
Dit quelque parolle cuisante,
S'elle n'ose, si le pense elle.

Povre je suis de ma jeunesse,
De povre et de petite extrace,
Mon pere n'eust oncq grant richesse
Ne son ayeul nommé Orace:
Povreté tous nous suit et trace,
Sur les tombeaulx de mes ancestres,
Les ames desquelz Dieu embrasse,
On n'y voit couronnes ne ceptres.

De povreté me garmentant
Souventesfois me dit le cuer,
"Homme, ne te doulouse tant
Et ne demaine tel douleur
Se tu n'as tant qu'eust Jaques Cuer,
Mieulx vault vivre soubz gros bureau
Povre, qu'avoir esté seigneur
Et pourrir soubz riche tombeau."

I've gone off on this digression
Which doesn't serve my purpose at all,
I am not a judge or deputy
For punishing or pardoning wrongs: *260*
I am the most imperfect of all,
Praised be the mild Jesus Christ,
Through me may they be satisfied,
What I have written is written. *264*

Let's leave the church where it lies
And talk of something more pleasant,
Not everyone likes this theme,
It's disagreeable and a bore: *268*
Peevish, whining Poverty
Rebellious and full of spite
Always throws in some cutting word
Or if she doesn't dare she thinks it. *272*

I've been poor from childhood on,
Of a humble, hard-pressed family,
My father never had much money
And neither did his father Horace: *276*
Poverty follows and tracks us all,
On the graves of my ancestors,
May God gather in their souls,
You won't see crowns or scepters. *280*

When I complain of being poor
My heart often tells me,
"You, man, don't be so depressed
And carry on so gloomily *284*
At not being as rich as Jacques Coeur,
Better to live under homespun
Poor, than to have once been a lord
And rot under a fancy stone." *288*

"Qu'avoir esté seigneur . . ." Que dis?
Seigneur, lasse, ne l'est il mais?
Selon les davitiques dis
"Son lieu ne congnoistra jamais":
Quant du surplus je m'en desmetz,
Il n'appartient a moy, pecheur,
Aux theologiens le remetz
Car c'est office de prescheur.

Si ne suis, bien le considere,
Filz d'ange portant dyademe
D'estoille ne d'autre sidere,
Mon pere est mort, Dieu en ait l'ame,
Quant est du corps il gist soubz lame,
J'entens que ma mere mourra,
El le scet bien, la povre femme,
Et le filz pas ne demourra.

Je congnois que povres et riches,
Sages et folz, prestres et laiz,
Nobles, villains, larges et chiches,
Petiz et grans, et beaulx et laiz,
Dames a rebrassez colletz
De quelconque condicion
Portans atours et bourreletz
Mort saisit sans excepcion.

Et meure Paris ou Helaine
Quiconques meurt meurt a douleur
Telle qu'il pert vent et alaine,
Son fiel se creve sur son cuer,
Puis sue Dieu scet quelle sueur
Et n'est qui de ses maux l'alege
Car enfant n'a, frere ne seur
Qui lors voulsist estre son plege.

"Have once been a lord . . ." What am I saying?
Lord, alas, isn't he one any more?
As it says in the Psalms of David
"His place shall not know him again": *292*
But I decline to go any further,
It's not my field, being a sinner,
I hand it back to the theologians
For it's a preacher's affair. *296*

I am not, I'm well aware,
An angel's son in a diadem
Of stars or constellations,
My father's dead, God keep his soul, *300*
His body lies under a stone,
My mother will die I understand
And she knows it too, poor woman,
And the son will not lag behind. *304*

I know that the poor and the rich,
The wise and the foolish, cleric and lay,
Nobles, villeins, the generous and the mean,
Big and little, handsome and homely, *308*
Ladies in folded-back collars,
No matter their worldly station
Wearing coverchiefs or cauls
Death seizes without exception. *312*

Be it Paris who dies or Helen
Whoever dies dies in such pain
The wind is knocked out of him,
His gall breaks on his heart, *316*
And he sweats God knows what sweat
And no one can relieve his pain,
For he hasn't child, brother, or sister
Willing to stand in for him then. *320*

La mort le fait fremir, pallir,
Le nez courber, les vaines tendre,
Le col enfler, la chair mollir,
Joinctes et nerfs croistre et estendre:
Corps femenin qui tant es tendre
Poly, souef, si precieux,
Te fauldra il ces maux attendre?
Oy, ou tout vif aller es cieulx.

BALLADE

Dictes moy ou, n'en quel pays,
Est Flora la belle Rommaine,
Archipiades ne Thaïs
Qui fut sa cousine germaine,
Echo parlant quant bruyt on maine
Dessus riviere ou sus estan
Qui beaulté ot trop plus qu'humaine?
Mais ou sont les neiges d'antan?

Ou est la tres sage Helloïs
Pour qui chastré fut et puis moyne
Pierre Esbaillart a Saint Denis,
Pour son amour ot ceste essoyne,
Semblablement ou est la royne
Qui commanda que Buridan
Fust geté en ung sac en Saine?
Mais ou sont les neiges d'antan?

La royne blanche comme lis
Qui chantoit a voix de seraine,
Berte au grant pié, Bietris, Alis,
Haremburgis qui tint le Maine
Et Jehanne la bonne Lorraine
Qu'Englois brulerent a Rouan,
Ou sont ilz, ou, Vierge souvraine?
Mais ou sont les neiges d'antan?

Death makes him shudder and blanch,
Makes his nostrils curl, his veins stand out,
His neck puff and flesh go limp,
Joints and sinews swell and stretch: *324*
O female body which is so precious
So smooth, delicate, and soft,
Will you too come to these agonies?
Yes, or rise in the flesh up to heaven. *328*

BALLADE

Tell me where, in what country,
Is Flora the beautiful Roman,
Archipiada or Thaïs
Who was first cousin to her once, *332*
Echo who speaks when there's a sound
On a pond or a river
Whose beauty was more than human?
But where are the snows of last year? *336*

Where is the learned Heloïse
For whom they castrated Pierre Abelard
And made him a monk at Saint-Denis,
For his love he took this pain, *340*
Likewise where is the queen
Who commanded that Buridan
Be thrown in a sack into the Seine?
But where are the snows of last year? *344*

The queen white as a lily
Who sang with a siren's voice,
Big-footed Bertha, Beatrice, Alice,
Haremburgis who held Maine *348*
And Jeanne the good maid of Lorraine
Whom the English burnt at Rouen, where,
Where are they, sovereign Virgin?
But where are the snows of last year? *352*

Prince, n'enquerrez de sepmaine
Ou elles sont, ne de cest an
Qu'a ce reffrain ne vous remaine,
Mais ou sont les neiges d'antan?

AUTRE BALLADE

Qui plus, ou est le tiers Calixte
Dernier decedé de ce nom
Qui quatre ans tint le papaliste,
Alphonce le roy d'Arragon,
Le gracieux duc de Bourbon
Et Artus le duc de Bretaigne
Et Charles septiesme le bon?
Mais ou est le preux Charlemaigne?

Semblablement le roy Scotiste
Qui demy face ot, ce dit on,
Vermeille comme une amatiste
Depuis le front jusqu'au menton,
Le roy de Chippre de renon,
Helas, et le bon roy d'Espaigne
Duquel je ne sçay pas le nom?
Mais ou est le preux Charlemaigne?

D'en plus parler je me desiste,
Le monde n'est qu'abusion,
Il n'est qui contre mort resiste
Ne qui treuve provision:
Encor fais une question,
Lancelot le roy de Behaigne,
Ou est il? Ou est son tayon?
Mais ou est le preux Charlemaigne?

Ou est Claquin le bon Breton,
Ou le conte Daulphin d'Auvergne
Et le bon feu duc d'Alençon?
Mais ou est le preux Charlemaigne?

Prince, you may not ask this week
Or this year where they are
That I will not give you this refrain,
But where are the snows of last year? *356*

ANOTHER BALLADE

And where's the third Callixtus
The last one to die of this name
Who four years held the papacy,
Alphonso the king of Aragon, *360*
The gracious duke of Bourbon
And Artus the duke of Bretagne
And Charles the Seventh the Good?
But where is the valiant Charlemagne? *364*

Similarly, the Scottish king
Half of whose face it is said
Was scarlet as an amethyst
From his forehead to his chin, *368*
The king of Cyprus of great renown,
Alas, and the good king of Spain
Whose name I can't remember?
But where is the valiant Charlemagne? *372*

There's no point in mentioning others,
This world is only a cheat,
Nobody can stave off death
Or get ready against it: *376*
Once more let me put a question,
Lancelot king of Behaigne,
Where is he? Where's his grandfather?
But where is the valiant Charlemagne? *380*

Where's Claquin the good Breton,
Or the count Dauphin of Auvergne
And the late good duke of Alençon?
But where is the valiant Charlemagne? *384*

AUTRE BALLADE

Car ou soit ly sains apostolles
D'aubes vestus, d'amys coeffez,
Qui ne saint fors saintes estolles
Dont par le col prent ly mauffez
De mal talant tout eschauffez,
Aussi bien meurt que cilz servans
De ceste vie cy bouffez,
Autant en emporte ly vens.

Voire, ou soit de Constantinobles
L'emperieres au poing dorez
Ou de France ly roy tres nobles
Sur tous autres roys decorez
Qui pour ly grans Dieux aourez
Bastist eglises et couvens,
S'en son temps il fut honnorez
Autant en emporte ly vens.

Ou soit de Vienne et de Grenobles
Ly Dauphin, ly preux, ly senez,
Ou de Dijon, Salins et Doles
Ly sires et ly filz ainsnez
Ou autant de leurs gens privez,
Heraulx, trompetes, poursuivans,
Ont ilz bien bouté soubz le nez?
Autant en emporte ly vens.

Princes a mort sont destinez
Et tous autres qui sont vivans,
S'ilz en sont courciez n'ataynez
Autant en emporte ly vens.

ANOTHER BALLADE

For be it His Holiness the Pope
In alb and amice all bedight,
Who girdeth on but his sacred stole
To seize the devil by the throat 388
All flaming with wicked will,
He dies in same wise as that lackey
From life here below puffed off,
This too the wind beareth away. 392

Yes, or be it the emperor
Of Constantinople with fist of gold
Or the most noble king of France
Foremost among all other kings 396
Who for the great adoréd God
Buildeth church and monastery,
If he had honor in his day
This too the wind beareth away. 400

Or be it of Vienne and Grenoble
The dauphin, the brave, the prudent,
Or of Dijon, Salins, and Dole
The great men and their eldest sons 404
Or an equal number of their servants,
Heralds, trumpeters, men-at-arms,
Did they not happily stuff their mugs?
This too the wind beareth away. 408

Princes are fated to die
And everyone else who's alive,
If they be angered by this or vexed
This too the wind beareth away. 412

LE TESTAMENT

Puis que papes, roys, filz de roys
Et conceus en ventres de roynes
Sont ensevelis mors et frois,
En autruy mains passent leurs regnes,
Moy povre mercerot de Renes
Mourray je pas? Oy, se Dieu plaist,
Mais que j'aye fait mes estrenes
Honneste mort ne me desplaist.

Ce monde n'est perpetuel
Quoy que pense riche pillart,
Tous sommes soubz mortel coutel,
Ce confort prent povre viellart
Lequel d'estre plaisant raillart
Ot le bruit lors que jeune estoit,
Qu'on tendroit a fol et paillart
Se viel a railler se mettoit.

Or luy convient il mendier
Car a ce force le contraint,
Regrete huy sa mort et hier,
Tristesse son cuer si estraint:
Se souvent, n'estoit Dieu qu'il craint,
Il feroit ung orrible fait
Et advient qu'en ce Dieu enfraint
Et que luy mesmes se desfait.

Car s'en jeunesse il fut plaisant
Ores plus riens ne dit qui plaise,
Tousjours viel cinge est desplaisant,
Moue ne fait qui ne desplaise:
S'il parle on luy dit qu'il se taise
Il est tenu pour fol recreu,
S'il parle on luy dit qu'il se taise
Et qu'en son prunier n'a pas creu.

Since popes, kings, and sons of kings
Conceived in wombs of queens
Are buried away dead and cold
And other hands assume their reigns, *416*
I a poor peddler from Rennes
Won't I die? Yes, if God so wishes,
But as long as I've sown my wild oats
An honest death won't displease me. *420*

The world will not last forever
Whatever the robber baron may think,
We all live under the mortal knife,
Thus the old timer consoles himself *424*
Who as the life of the party
Was famous when he was young
And who'd be thought cracked and lewd
If old he started poking fun. *428*

Now it's his lot to go begging
For necessity obliges it,
Day after day he longs for death
Sadness so clutches his heart: *432*
Often but for the fear of God
He'd commit a horrible deed
And so it would happen he'd break God's law
And do away with himself. *436*

For if in his youth he was funny
Now nothing he says can get a laugh,
An old monkey's always unpleasant
And every face he makes is ugly: *440*
If trying to please he keeps quiet
Everybody thinks he's gone senile,
If he speaks they tell him to be still,
That plum didn't grow on his own tree. *444*

Aussi ces povres fameletes
Qui vielles sont et n'ont de quoy,
Quant ilz voient ces pucelletes
Emprunter elles a requoy
Ilz demandent a Dieu pourquoy
Si tost naquirent, n'a quel droit?
Nostre Seigneur se taist tout quoy
Car au tancer il le perdroit.

Advis m'est que j'oy regreter
La belle qui fut hëaulmiere
Soy jeune fille soushaitter
Et parler en telle maniere:
"Ha, vieillesse felonne et fiere,
Pourquoi m'as si tost abatue?
Qui me tient, qui, que ne me fiere
Et qu'a ce coup je ne me tue?

"Tollu m'as la haulte franchise
Que beaulté m'avoit ordonné
Sur clers, marchans et gens d'Eglise
Car lors il n'estoit homme né
Qui tout le sien ne m'eust donné,
Quoy qu'il en fust des repentailles,
Mais que luy eusse habandonné
Ce que reffusent truandailles.

"A maint homme l'ay reffusé
Qui n'estoit a moy grant sagesse
Pour l'amour d'ung garson rusé
Auquel j'en feiz grande largesse:
A qui que je feisse finesse,
Par m'ame, je l'amoye bien
Or ne me faisoit que rudesse
Et ne m'amoit que pour le mien.

The same with the poor old women
Who've grown old and haven't a penny,
When they see the young girls
Squeezing them out on the sly 448
They demand of God how it is,
By what right, they were born so soon?
Our Lord shuts up and keeps quiet
For in a scolding-match with them He'd lose. 452

It seems I can hear the complaint
Of the beauty who used to be helmeter
Wishing she were a girl again
And she's saying something like this: 456
"Ah false, insolent old age,
Why did you beat me down so early?
What holds me, what, from striking myself
And killing myself with a blow? 460

"You've taken from me the high hand
That beauty ordained was mine
Over clerks, merchants, men of the Church
For once there wasn't a man born 464
Who wouldn't have given all he owned,
Repent it as he might later on,
If I'd have just let him have
What now the tramps won't take for free. 468

"To plenty of men I refused it
Which wasn't very smart of me
For the love of a smooth operator
Whom I gave free play with it: 472
So what if I fooled around?
I swear I loved him truly
But he just gave me a hard time
And only loved me for my money. 476

"Si ne me sceut tant detrayner,
Fouler aux piez, que ne l'aymasse
Et m'eust il fait les rains trayner
S'il m'eust dit que je le baisasse
Que tous mes maulx je n'oubliasse,
Le glouton de mal entechié
M'embrassoit, j'en suis bien plus grasse,
Que m'en reste il? Honte et pechié.

"Or est il mort passé trente ans
Et je remains vielle, chenue,
Quant je pense, lasse, au bon temps,
Quelle fus, quelle devenue,
Quant me regarde toute nue
Et je me voy si tres changiee,
Povre, seiche, megre, menue,
Je suis presque toute enragiee.

"Qu'est devenu ce front poly,
Cheveulx blons, ces sourcils voultiz,
Grant entroeil, ce regart joly
Dont prenoie les plus soubtilz,
Ce beau nez droit grant ne petiz,
Ces petites joinctes oreilles,
Menton fourchu, cler vis traictiz
Et ces belles levres vermeilles?

"Ces gentes espaulles menues,
Ces bras longs et ces mains traictisses,
Petiz tetins, hanches charnues,
Eslevees, propres, faictisses
A tenir amoureuses lisses,
Ces larges rains, ce sadinet
Assis sur grosses fermes cuisses
Dedens son petit jardinet?

"He could wipe the floor with me,
Or kick me, he couldn't kill my love,
Even if he'd broken my back
He'd only have to ask a kiss *480*
And my troubles would disappear,
The glutton wicked to the bone
Would take me in his arms—a lot I gained—
What have I left? The shame and sin. *484*

"He's been dead these thirty years
And I stay on old and grizzled,
When I think, alas, of the happy times,
What I was, what I've become, *488*
When I look at myself naked
And see myself so terribly changed,
Poor, dried up, lean and bony,
I nearly go off my head. *492*

"What has become of that bright forehead,
That yellow hair, those arched eyebrows,
The wide-set eyes, the pretty glance
Which bewitched the slyest of men, *496*
The fine, straight nose not too big or small,
Those small ears pressed close to the head,
The dimpled chin, the clear oval face
And the lips beautiful and red? *500*

"Those delicate little shoulders,
The long arms and slender hands,
The small breasts, the full buttocks
High, fit, and well-designed *504*
For holding the jousts of love,
Those wide loins, and that pussy
Set between thick, firm thighs
In its own little flower garden? *508*

"Le front ridé, les cheveux gris,
Les sourcilz cheus, les yeulx estains
Qui faisoient regars et ris
Dont mains meschans furent attains,
Nez courbes de beaulté loingtains,
Oreilles pendantes, moussues,
Le vis pally, mort et destains,
Menton froncé, levres peaussues.

"C'est d'umaine beaulté l'issue,
Les bras cours et les mains contraites,
Les espaulles toutes bossues,
Mamelles, quoy? toutes retraites,
Telles les hanches que les tetes,
Du sadinet, fy! quant des cuisses
Cuisses ne sont plus mais cuissetes
Grivelees comme saulcisses.

"Ainsi le bon temps regretons
Entre nous, povres vielles sotes
Assises bas a crouppetons
Tout en ung tas comme pelotes
A petit feu de chenevotes
Tost allumees, tost estaintes,
Et jadis fusmes si mignotes,
Ainsi en prent a mains et maintes."

BALLADE

"Or y pensez belle Gantiere
Qui m'escoliere souliez estre
Et vous Blanche la Savetiere,
Or est il temps de vous congnoistre:
Prenez a destre et a senestre,
N'espargnez homme, je vous prie,
Car vielles n'ont ne cours ne estre
Ne que monnoye qu'on descrie.

"The forehead lined, the hair gray,
The brows dropped out, the eyes filmy
Which used to cast those smiles and glances
That got to many a poor devil, *512*
The nose hooked far from beauty,
The ears hanging loose and sprouting moss,
The face washed out, dead, and pasty,
The chin furrowed, the lips just skin, *516*

"This is how human beauty comes out,
The arms short, the hands shriveled,
The shoulders up in a hunch,
The breasts? shrunk in again, *520*
The buttocks gone the way of the tits,
The hole? agh! as for the thighs
They aren't thighs at all but sticks
Speckled all over like sausages. *524*

"This is how we lament the good old days
Among ourselves, poor silly crones
Dumped down on our haunches
All in a heap like so many skeins *528*
Around a tiny hempstalk fire
No sooner lighted than out
And once we were so adorable,
So it goes for men and women." *532*

BALLADE

"Now think a bit beautiful glover
Who used to be my apprentice
And you Blanche the shoe-fitter,
It's time you knew what you're worth: *536*
Grab what you can left and right,
Don't spare a man, I beg you,
For there's no run on old crones
No more than cried-down money. *540*

"Et vous la gente Saulciciere
Qui de dancier estre adestre,
Guillemete la Tapiciere,
Ne mesprenez vers vostre maistre:
Tost vous fauldra clorre fenestre
Quant deviendrez vielle, flestrie,
Plus ne servirez qu'ung viel prestre
Ne que monnoye qu'on descrie.

"Jehanneton la Chapperonniere
Gardez qu'amy ne vous empestre
Et Katherine la Bourciere
N'envoyez plus les hommes paistre,
Car qui belle n'est ne perpetre
Leur male grace mais leur rie,
Laide viellesse amour n'empestre
Ne que monnoye qu'on descrie.

"Filles, vueillez vous entremettre
D'escouter pourquoy pleure et crie,
Pour ce que je ne me puis mettre
Ne que monnoye qu'on descrie."

Ceste leçon icy leur baille
La belle et bonne de jadis,
Bien dit ou mal, vaille que vaille,
Enregistrer j'ay faict ces dis
Par mon clerc Fremin l'estourdis,
Aussi rassis que je pense estre,
S'il me desment je le mauldis,
Selon le clerc est deu le maistre.

"And you sweet sausage-filler
With such a flair for the dance
And Guillemette weaver of rugs,
Make no mistake of who's your master: *544*
Soon you'll have to close up shop
When you've become old and baggy,
You'll be good for no one but an old priest
No more than cried-down money. *548*

"Jeanneton maker of bonnets
Don't let a lover hold you back
And Catherine vender of purses,
Stop sending your men to pasture, *552*
A girl who's no beauty shouldn't
Vex them, but should make them laugh,
Foul old age doesn't get any love
No more than cried-down money. *556*

"Girls, would you stop a minute
And let it sink in why I weep and cry,
I can't get into circulation
No more than cried-down money." *560*

This lesson is given them by her
Who was once beautiful and good,
Well said or not, for what it's worth,
I've had the speech copied down *564*
By my clerk Fremin the dimwit,
As sound of mind as I'll ever be,
If he denies it I'll curse him out,
The master's made by the clerk. *568*

Si aperçoy le grant dangier
Ouquel homme amoureux se boute,
Et qui me vouldroit laidangier
De ce mot, en disant, "Escoute,
Se d'amer t'estrange et reboute
Le barat de celles nommees
Tu fais une bien folle doubte
Car ce sont femmes diffamees.

"S'ilz n'ayment fors que pour l'argent
On ne les ayme que pour l'eure,
Rondement ayment toute gent
Et rient lors quant bourse pleure,
De celles cy n'est qui ne queure,
Mais en femmes d'onneur et nom
Franc homme, se Dieu me sequeure,
Se doit emploier, ailleurs non."

Je prens qu'aucun dye cecy
Si ne me contente il en rien,
En effect il conclut ainsy
Et je le cuide entendre bien
Qu'on doit amer en lieu de bien,
Assavoir mon se ces filletes
Qu'en parolles toute jour tien
Ne furent ilz femmes honnestes?

Honnestes si furent vraiement
Sans avoir reproches ne blasmes,
Si est vray qu'au commencement
Une chascune de ces femmes
Lors prindrent, ains qu'eussent diffames,
L'une ung clerc, ung lay, l'autre ung moine,
Pour estaindre d'amours les flammes
Plus chauldes que feu saint Antoine.

From this I can see the great danger
A man in love gets himself into,
Someone may want to take me to task
For these words, saying, "Listen, *572*
If you're disgusted, thrown off love
By the slippery dealings of those you've named
Your misgiving is plain silly
For these are women of ill-repute. *576*

"If they only make love for money
One only loves them for the hour,
Heartily they love everybody
And laugh when a purse bursts in tears, *580*
Every last one of them runs around,
With women of good name and honor
An upright man, so help me God,
Should take up, and not with others." *584*

Suppose that someone says all this,
He doesn't impress me one bit,
In effect he draws the conclusion
And I think I get his meaning right *588*
You should love in respectable circles
But I'd like to know if these wenches
With whom all day long I make talk
Weren't themselves virtuous women once? *592*

Virtuous they were for a fact
Without any reproach or blame,
It's a fact too that at the start
Each of these women in turn *596*
Took in before she got her bad name,
One a clerk, one a layman, another a friar,
Trying to stamp out love's flames
Hotter than Saint Anthony's Fire. *600*

Or firent selon le decret
Leurs amys, et bien y appert,
Ilz amoient en lieu secret
Car autre d'eulx n'y avoit part:
Toutesfois, celle amour se part
Car celle qui n'en amoit qu'un
De celuy s'eslongne et despart
Et aime mieulx amer chascun.

Qui les meut a ce? J'ymagine,
San l'onneur des dames blasmer,
Que c'est nature femenine
Qui tout unyement veult amer,
Autre chose n'y sçay rimer
Fors qu'on dit a Rains et a Troys,
Voire a l'Isle et a Saint Omer,
Que six ouvriers font plus que trois.

Or ont ces folz amans le bont
Et les dames prins la vollee,
C'est le droit loyer qu'amans ont,
Toute foy y est viollee
Quelque doulx baisier n'acollee,
"De chiens, d'oyseaulx, d'armes, d'amours,"
Chascun le dit a la vollee,
"Pour ung plaisir mille doulours."

DOUBLE BALLADE

Pour ce amez tant que vouldrez,
Suyvez assemblees et festes,
En la fin ja mieulx n'en vauldrez
Et n'y romperez que vos testes:
Folles amours font le gens bestes,
Salmon en ydolatria,
Samson en perdit ses lunetes,
Bien est eureux qui riens n'y a.

Now by the decree their lovers
Abided, so it really appears,
They conducted their affairs in private
And nobody else was in on it: *604*
And yet in time this love breaks up
For she who only loved one of them
Gives him the slip and seeks abroad
And gets to love loving them all. *608*

What makes them do it? I imagine,
Without impugning female honor,
It is the nature of woman
To want to love all men at once, *612*
Other reasons I can't put in poetry
Except they say at Rheims and Troyes,
Also at Lille and Saint-Omer,
Six workmen do more work than three. *616*

Now these poor simps get the bounce
And the ladies have taken the volley,
This is the lover's one return,
Here every vow is broken *620*
For all the sweet kisses and hugs,
"In dogs, falconry, arms, and love,"
Everybody tosses it off,
"For one joy a thousand sorrows." *624*

DOUBLE BALLADE

And therefore love all you want,
Go to assemblages and feasts,
In the end you'll be no better off
And all you can break is your heads: *628*
Mad love changes men into beasts,
It made an idolater of Solomon,
And through it Samson lost his orbs,
Lucky is he who has no part of it. *632*

Orpheüs le doux menestrier
Jouant de fleustes et musetes
En fut en dangier d'un murtrier
Chien Cerberus a quatre testes:
Et Narcisus le bel honnestes
En ung parfont puis se noya
Pour l'amour de ses amouretes,
Bien est eureux qui riens n'y a.

Sardana le preux chevalier
Qui conquist le regne de Cretes
En voulut devenir moullier
Et filler entre pucelletes:
David le roy, sage prophetes,
Crainte de Dieu en oublia
Voyant laver cuisses bien faites,
Bien est eureux qui riens n'y a.

Amon en voult deshonnourer
Faignant de menger tarteletes
Sa seur Thamar et desflourer
Qui fut inceste deshonnestes:
Herodes, pas ne sont sornetes,
Saint Jehan Baptiste en decola
Pour dances, saulx et chansonnetes,
Bien est eureux qui riens n'y a.

De moy, povre, je vueil parler,
J'en fus batu comme a ru telles
Tout nu, ja ne le quier celer,
Qui me feist maschier ces groselles
Fors Katherine de Vausselles?
Noel le tiers est qui fut la,
Mitaines a ces nopces telles,
Bien est eureux qui riens n'y a.

The dulcet minstrel Orpheus
Playing his flutes and pipes
For love braved the bloodthirsty
Dog the four-headed Cerberus: *636*
The beautiful boy Narcissus
Got drowned way down in a well
For the love of his lovelies,
Lucky is he who has no part of it. *640*

Sardana the valiant knight
Who conquered the kingdom of Crete
For love wanted to be a woman
And join the virgins' spinning set: *644*
King David the wise prophet
Through love forgot his fear of God
Seeing shapely thighs in the bath,
Lucky is he who has no part of it. *648*

It made Amnon wish to dishonor
On the pretext of eating tarts
His sister Tamar and deflower her
Which was disgraceful incest: *652*
Herod, and this is not in fun,
Cut off John the Baptist's head
For dances, tumbles, and croonings,
Lucky is he who has no part of it. *656*

Of my poor self let me say
I was drubbed like laundry in a brook
Bare-assed, no need to hide it,
Who made me down this sour mash *660*
But Katherine of Vausselles?
Noël was the third one there,
May he get as banged at his nuptials,
Lucky is he who has no part of it. *664*

Mais que ce jeune bacheler
Laissast ces jeunes bacheletes?
Non, et le deust on vif brusler
Comme ung chevaucheur d'escouvetes:
Plus doulces luy sont que civetes
Mais toutesfoys fol s'y fya,
Soient blanches, soient brunetes,
Bien est eureux qui riens n'y a.

Se celle que jadis servoie
De si bon cuer et loyaument
Dont tant de maulx et griefz j'avoie
Et souffroie tant de torment
Se dit m'eust au commencement
Sa voulenté (mais nennil, las)
J'eusse mis paine aucunement
De moy retraire de ses las.

Quoy que je luy voulsisse dire
Elle estoit preste d'escouter
Sans m'acorder ne contredire,
Qui plus, me souffroit acouter
Joignant d'elle, pres sacouter
Et ainsi m'aloit amusant
Et me souffroit tout raconter
Mais ce n'estoit qu'en m'abusant.

Abusé m'a et fait entendre
Tousjours d'ung que ce fust ung aultre,
De farine que ce fust cendre,
D'ung mortier ung chappeau de faultre,
De viel machefer que fust peaultre,
D'ambesars que ce fussent ternes
(Tousjours trompeur autruy enjaultre
Et rent vecies pour lanternes).

But would this young bachelor
Give up the young bachelorettes?
No, not even if he had to burn
Like those who ride the broomsticks, *668*
They are sweeter to him than civet
But every time the fool got taken:
Whether she's blonde or brunette,
Lucky is he who has no part of it. *672*

If she whom I used to serve
So eagerly and faithfully
For which I got such pain and wrong
And went through such torment *676*
Only had told me at the start
Her wishes (but not a chance)
I'd have managed somehow or other
To get myself free of her snares. *680*

No matter what I wanted to say
She was always ready to listen
Without giving in, or saying no,
She'd even let me come so near *684*
We'd touch as I sighed in her ear
And in this way she led me on
And got me to pour out my heart
But it was just to make a fool of me. *688*

She fooled me all right, led me to think
Everything always was something else,
That wheat flour was potash,
A mortar board a felt hat, *692*
Old furnace slag really pewter,
And snake-eyes double trey
(The smoothie can always gull you
And foist off bladders as lanterns). *696*

Du ciel une poille d'arain,
Des nues une peau de veau,
Du matin qu'estoit le serain,
D'ung trongnon de chou ung naveau,
D'orde cervoise vin nouveau,
D'une truie ung molin a vent
Et d'une hart ung escheveau,
D'ung gras abbé ung poursuyvant.

Ainsi m'ont Amours abusé
Et pourmené de l'uys au pesle,
Je croy qu'homme n'est si rusé
Fust fin comme argent de coepelle
Qui n'y laissast linge, drappelle
Mais qu'il fust ainsi manyé
Comme moy, qui partout m'appelle
L'amant remys et regnyé.

Je regnie amours et despite
Et deffie a feu et a sang,
Mort par elles me precipite
Et ne leur en chault pas d'ung blanc:
Ma vïelle ay mys subz le banc,
Amans ne suiveray jamais,
Se jadis je fus de leur ranc
Je desclare que n'en suis mais.

Car j'ay mys le plumail au vent,
Or le suyve qui a attente,
De ce me tais doresnavant
Car poursuivre vueil mon entente,
Et s'aucun m'interroge ou tente
Comment d'amours j'ose mesdire
Ceste parolle le contente,
Qui meurt, a ses loix de tout dire.

The sky a copper frying pan,
The clouds really calfskins,
The morning the evening,
A cabbage stump a turnip, *700*
Rotgut beer brand new wine,
A battering ram a windmill
And a noose a hank of yarn,
A fat priest a man-at-arms. *704*

In this way love made me the fool,
Lured me out and threw the bolt,
I think no man lives crafty enough
Were he subtle as finest silver *708*
Who wouldn't have lost his shirt and drawers
If he'd been handled in the same manner
As me, whom everybody calls
The jilted and rejected lover. *712*

I renounce and despise love
And defy it in fire and blood,
With such women death bundles me off
And they couldn't care less: *716*
I've stowed my fiddle under the bench,
I'll give up the company of lovers,
If I used to be in their ranks
I declare now I am no longer. *720*

I thrust my feather to the wind,
Let him who has the time go chase it,
I'll shut up on this from now on
For I want to get back to the project: *724*
If someone questions or quizzes me
On how I dare to run love down
Let him make do with this answer,
A dying man can lay it on the line. *728*

Je congnois approcher ma seuf,
Je crache blanc comme coton
Jacoppins gros comme ung esteuf,
Qu'esse a dire? que Jehanneton
Plus ne me tient pour valeton
Mais pour ung viel usé roquart,
De viel porte voix et le ton
Et ne suys qu'ung jeune coquart.

Dieu mercy et Tacque Thibault
Qui tant d'eaue froide m'a fait boire
Mis en bas lieu non pas en hault,
Mengier d'angoisse mainte poire,
Enferré: quant j'en ay memoire
Je prie pour luy *et reliqua*
Que Dieu luy doint, et voire, voire,
Ce que je pense, *et cetera.*

Toutesfois je n'y pense mal
Pour luy et pour son lieutenant,
Aussi pour son official
Qui est plaisant et advenant:
Que faire n'ay du remenant
Mais du petit maistre Robert,
Je les ayme tout d'ung tenant
Ainsi que fait Dieu le Lombart.

Si me souvient bien, Dieu mercis,
Que je feis a mon partement
Certains laiz, l'an cinquante six,
Qu'aucuns sans mon consentement
Voulurent nommer testament,
Leur plaisir fut non pas le mien,
Mais quoy? On dit communement
Qu'ung chascun n'est maistre du sien.

I feel my thirst coming on,
I spit white as cotton
Clams the size of a tennis ball,
What's there to say? that Jeanneton 732
Won't see me as a boy any more
But as an old broken down drayhorse,
Like an old geezer I wheeze and crack
And I'm still a young whippersnapper. 736

Thanks to God and Tacque Thibault
Who made me drink all that cold water
Thrust in a dungeon not upstairs
And eat all those choke-pears 740
In irons: when it comes back to me
I pray for him *et reliqua*
That God may give him, exactly,
What I have in mind, *et cetera.* 744

And yet I harbor no ill will
Against him or his lieutenant,
The same goes for his official
Who's outgoing and pleasant: 748
I've had no truck with the rest
Except for little Master Robert,
I love them all of a piece
Just the way God loves the Lombard. 752

I haven't forgotten, thank God,
That I composed on my departure
Certain legacies, in fifty-six,
That some without my consent 756
Have wanted to call a testament,
This was their idea not mine,
But so what? As the saying goes,
Nobody's master of his own. 760

Pour les revoquer ne le dis
Et y courust toute ma terre,
De pitié ne suis refroidis
Envers le Bastart de la Barre:
Parmi ses trois gluyons de fuerre
Je luy donne mes vieilles nates,
Bonnes seront pour tenir serre
Et soy soustenir sur les pates.

S'ainsi estoit qu'aucun n'eust pas
Receu le laiz que je luy mande
J'ordonne qu'après mon trespas
A mes hoirs en face demande,
Mais qui sont ils? S'i le demande,
Moreau, Provins, Robin Turgis,
De moy, dictes que je leur mande,
Ont eu jusqu'au lit ou je gis.

Somme, plus ne diray qu'ung mot
Car commencer vueil a tester,
Devant mon clerc Fremin qui m'ot
S'il ne dort, je vueil protester
Que n'entens homme detester
En ceste presente ordonnance
Et ne la vueil magnifester
Si non ou royaume de France.

Je sens mon cuer qui s'affoiblit
Et plus je ne puis papier,
Fremin sié toy pres de mon lit
Que l'on ne me viengne espier,
Prens ancre tost, plume, papier,
Ce que nomme escry vistement,
Puys fay le partout coppier,
Et vecy le commancement.

It isn't to take them back I mention them
Though all I own might be at stake,
I haven't grown cold-hearted
Toward the Bastard of the Bar: *764*
Along with his three bundles of straw
I give him my old floor mats,
They'll be good for getting a grip
And keeping himself up on all fours. *768*

If it turns out that anyone
Didn't get the bequest I made him
I decree that after I've passed on
He raise the matter with my heirs, *772*
But who are they? If he should ask,
It's Moreau, Provins, Robin Turgis
Who from me, you can say I said so,
Got it all right down to the bed I'm on. *776*

Now I'll say just one more thing
For I'd like to start on the will,
Before my clerk Fremin who's listening
If he's not asleep, I wish to state *780*
I intend to cut off no one
In this present disposition
And that I don't want it published
If not in the kingdom of France. *784*

I can feel my heart giving out,
I can't keep rambling on this way,
Fremin sit here close by the bed
So no one can come in and spy on me, *788*
Hurry, get ink, pen, paper,
What I dictate write down at once,
Then get copies made everywhere,
And here is the beginning. *792*

Ou nom de Dieu, Pere eternel,
Et du Filz que vierge parit,
Dieu au Pere coeternel
Ensemble et le Saint Esperit
Qui sauva ce qu'Adam perit
Et du pery pare les cieulx,
Qui bien ce croit peu ne merit,
Gens mors estre faiz petiz dieux.

Mors estoient et corps et ames
En dampnee perdicion,
Corps pourris et ames en flammes
De quelconque condicion:
Toutesfois, fais excepcion
Des patriarches et prophetes
Car selon ma concepcion
Oncques n'eurent grant chault aux fesses.

Qui me diroit, "Qui vous fait metre
Si tres avant ceste parolle
Qui n'estes en theologie maistre?
A vous est presumpcion folle,"
C'est de Jhesus la parabolle
Touchant du Riche ensevely
En feu non pas en couche molle
Et du Ladre de dessus ly.

Se du Ladre eust veu le doit ardre
Ja n'en eust requis refrigere
N'eaue au bout de ses dois aherdre
Pour rafreschir sa maschouëre:
Pyons y feront mate chiere
Qui boyvent pourpoint et chemise
Puis que boiture y est si chiere,
Dieu nous en gart, bourde jus mise.

In the name of God, eternal Father,
And of the Son born of virgin,
God co-eternal with the Father
And with the Holy Ghost 796
Who saved those whom Adam lost
And adorns heaven with the dead,
It's not easy to believe
Dead people are made little gods. 800

Dead they were body and soul
In damned perdition,
Bodies rotted and souls in flame
Whatever their worldly station: 804
To be sure I'm not including
The patriarchs and the prophets
For according to my idea
These never got their asses burned. 808

If someone should say, "What makes you
Put forward this view so boldly
When you're not even master of theology?
Your presumption's incredible," 812
The answer is Jesus' parable
Of the rich man who was laid out
In fire instead of a soft bed
And of Lazarus up above him. 816

If he had seen Lazarus' finger burn
Then he wouldn't have asked for it to cool him
Or for water at that fingertip
To refresh his throat: 820
The drunks will really grouse down there
Who drink the shirt off their backs
If the price of booze is that high,
God keep us from this, joking aside. 824

Ou nom de Dieu comme j'ay dit
Et de sa glorieuse Mere
Sans pechié soit parfait ce dit
Par moy plus megre que chimere:
Se je n'ay eu fievre eufumere
Ce m'a fait divine clemence
Mais d'autre dueil et perte amere
Je me tais et ainsi commence.

Premier, doue de ma povre ame
La glorieuse Trinité
Et la commande a Nostre Dame,
Chambre de la divinité,
Priant toute la charité
Des dignes neuf Ordres des cieulx
Que par eulx soit ce don porté
Devant le Trosne precieux.

Item, mon corps j'ordonne et laisse
A nostre grant mere la terre,
Les vers n'y trouveront grant gresse
Trop luy a fait fain dure guerre:
Or luy soit delivré grant erre,
De terre vint, en terre tourne,
Toute chose se par trop n'erre
Voulentiers en son lieu retourne.

Item, et a mon plus que pere
Maistre Guillaume de Villon
Qui esté m'a plus doulx que mere
A enfant levé de maillon,
Degeté m'a de maint bouillon
Et de cestuy pas ne s'esjoye,
Si luy requier a genouillon
Qu'il me'en laisse toute la joye,

In the name of God as I said
And of His glorious Mother
Sinlessly may this work be done
By me skinnier than a madman: *828*
If I escaped the cholera
It was by clemency divine
But of other bitter griefs and loss
I say nothing and so begin. *832*

First, I bestow my poor soul
On the Blessed Trinity
And commend it to Our Lady,
Chamber of Divinity *836*
Beseeching all the charity
Of the nine high Orders of Heaven
That they may take this offering
Before the precious Throne. *840*

Item, I give and leave my body
To the Earth our great mother,
The worms won't find much meat on it
So fiercely did hunger make war: *844*
Let it quickly be given her,
From earth it came, to earth it goes,
All things unless they stray too far
Gladly return to their own place. *848*

Item, to my more than father
Master Guillaume de Villon
Who has been gentler to me than mother
To child just out of swaddling clothes, *852*
He has saved me from many a jam
And isn't enjoying the one I'm in now,
I beg of him on bended knee
To leave all the joy of it to me, *856*

Je luy donne ma librairie
Et le Rommant du Pet au Deable
Lequel maistre Guy Tabarie
Grossa, qui est homs veritable:
Par cayers est soubz une table,
Combien qu'il soit rudement fait
La matiere est si tres notable
Qu'elle amende tout le mesfait.

Item, donne a ma povre mere
Pour saluer nostre Maistresse
Qui pour moy ot douleur amere,
Dieu le scet, et mainte tristesse,
Autre chastel n'ay ne fortresse
Ou me retraye corps ne ame
Quant sur moy court malle destresse,
Ne ma mere, la povre femme:

BALLADE

Dame du ciel, regente terrienne,
Emperiere des infernaux palus,
Recevez moy vostre humble chrestienne
Que comprinse soye entre vos esleus
Ce non obstant qu'oncques rien ne valus:
Les biens de vous, ma Dame et ma Maistresse,
Sont trop plus grans que ne suis pecheresse
Sans lesquelz biens ame ne peut merir
N'avoir les cieulx, je n'en suis jangleresse,
En ceste foy je vueil vivre et mourir.

A vostre Filz dictes que je suis sienne,
De luy soyent mes pechiez abolus,
Pardonne moy comme a l'Egipcienne
Ou comme il feist au clerc Theophilus
Lequel par vous fut quitte et absolus

I give him my library
And *The Tale of the Devil's Fart*
Which Master Guy Tabary
Reproduced, who's a truthful fellow: *860*
It's laid in heaps under a table,
The style may be a little crude
But the matter's so overpowering
It makes up for all the defects. *864*

Item, I give my poor mother
To salute Our Lady with,
Who suffered bitterly for me,
God knows, and had many heartaches, *868*
I've no other castle or fortress
Where body or soul can find haven
When real trouble runs me down,
Nor has my mother, poor woman: *872*

BALLADE

Lady of heaven, regent of earth,
Empress over the swamps of hell,
Receive me your humble Christian
That I may be counted among your elect,
This even though I was never of worth: *877*
Your bounties, my Lady and my Mistress,
Are greater by far than my sinfulness
And without them no soul could merit
Or enter heaven, I'm not pretending now,
In this faith I wish to live and to die. *882*

Tell your Son that I belong to Him,
Through Him let my sins be washed away,
May He pardon me like the Egyptian woman
Or as He did Theophilus the clerk
Who through you was acquitted and absolved *887*

Combien qu'il eust au deable fait promesse,
Preservez moy que ne face jamais ce,
Vierge portant sans rompture encourir
Le sacrement qu'on celebre a la messe,
En ceste foy je vueil vivre et mourir.

Femme je suis povrette et ancïenne
Qui riens ne sçay, oncques lettre ne lus,
Au moustier voy dont suis paroissienne
Paradis paint ou sont harpes et lus
Et ung enfer ou dampnez sont boullus:
L'ung me fait paour, l'autre joye et liesse,
La joye avoir me fay, haulte Deesse,
A qui pecheurs doivent tous recourir
Comblez de foy, sans fainte ne paresse,
En ceste foy je vueil vivre et mourir.

Vous portastes, digne Vierge, princesse,
Iesus regnant qui n'a ne fin ne cesse,
Le Tout Puissant prenant nostre foiblesse
Laissa les cieulx et nous vint secourir,
Offrit a mort sa tres chiere jeunesse,
Nostre Seigneur tel est, tel le confesse,
En ceste foy je vueil vivre et mourir.

Item, m'amour, ma chiere Rose,
Ne luy laisse ne cuer ne foye,
Elle ameroit mieulx autre chose
Combien qu'elle ait assez monnoye:
Quoy? une grant bource de soye
Plaine d'escuz, parfonde et large,
Mais pendu soit il, que je soye,
Qui luy laira escu ne targe.

Car elle en a sans moy assez
Mais de cela il ne m'en chault,
Mes plus grans dueilz en sont passez
Plus n'en ay le croppion chault:

Although he had compacted with the devil,
Preserve me from ever doing this,
Virgin who bore with hymen unbroken
The sacrament we celebrate at Mass,
In this faith I wish to live and to die. *892*

I'm just a poor old lady,
Who knows nothing and can't read a word,
At my own parish church I see
A painted paradise with harps and lutes
And a hell where they boil the damned, *897*
One scares me, one gives me joy and bliss,
Let mine be the joyful one, high Goddess,
On whom all sinners must rely
Brimming with faith, without sham or sloth,
In this faith I wish to live and to die. *902*

Virgin so worthy, princess, you bore
Iesus reigning without end or term,
Lord Almighty who took up our weakness
Left his heaven and came for our succor,
Offered to death His precious youth,
Now is Our Lord, so I acknowledge Him,
In this faith I wish to live and to die. *909*

Item, to my love, my dear Rose,
I don't leave my heart or liver either,
There's something she craves even more
And she isn't hard up for money: *913*
What can it be? A big silk purse
Swollen with *écus,* long and large,
But may the man hang, and me too,
Who slips her his *écu* or his *targe.* *917*

For she gets it enough without me
But this doesn't rile me up,
My worst griefs have all gone by
And I no longer get it up: *921*

Si m'en desmetz aux hoirs Michault
Qui fut nommé le Bon Fouterre,
Priez pour luy, faictes ung sault,
A Saint Satur gist, soubz Sancerre.

Ce non obstant, pour m'acquitter
Envers amours plus qu'envers elle,
Car onques n'y peuz acquester
D'espoir une seule estincelle,
Je ne sçay s'a tous si rebelle
A esté, ce m'est grant esmoy,
Mais, par sainte Marie la belle,
Je n'y voy que rire pour moy,

Ceste ballade luy envoye
Qui se termine tout par erre,
Qui luy portera? Que je voye,
Ce sera Pernet de la Barre,
Pourveu s'il rencontre en son erre
Ma damoiselle au nez tortu
Il luy dira sans plus enquerre,
"Orde paillarde, dont viens tu?"

BALLADE

Faulse beauté qui tant me couste chier,
Rude en effect, ypocrite doulceur,
Amour dure plus que fer a maschier,
Nommer que puis, de ma desfaçon seur,
Cherme felon, la mort d'ung povre cuer,
Orgueil mussié qui gens met au mourir,
Yeulx sans pitié, ne veult Droit de Rigueur
Sans empirer ung povre secourir?

Mieulx m'eust valu avoir esté serchier
Ailleurs secours, c'eust esté mon onneur,
Riens ne m'eust sceu lors de ce fait hachier,
Trotter m'en fault en fuyte et deshonneur,
Haro, haro, le grant et le mineur!
Et qu'esse cy? Mourray sans coup ferir?
Ou Pitié veult, selon ceste teneur,
Sans empirer ung povre secourir?

I stand down for the heirs of Michault
Who was nicknamed the Great Fucker,
Say prayers for him, then take a tumble,
He lies at Saint-Satur, below Sancerre. *925*

Nevertheless, to settle up
With love rather than with her,
For never did she let me have
Even a little spark of hope, *929*
I don't know if she was as difficult
With all men, and this made me suffer,
But, by Saint Mary the Beautiful,
There's nothing in it but a laugh for me, *933*

I send her this *ballade*
In which all the lines end in "R,"
Who'll deliver it? Let me see,
It shall be Perrenet of the Bar, *937*
Provided if he meet on the way
My damsel with the nose pushed in
He say without further ado,
"Dirty tramp, where've you been?" *941*

BALLADE

False beauty who makes me pay so dear,
Harsh in fact, falsely tender,
A love harder to chew than an iron bar,
Whom I can name, sure now of my disaster, *945*
Deceiving charm, death of a heart so poor,
Secret pride that drives men to despair,
Pitiless eyes—will not Justice with Rigor
Cure a poor wretch without making him sicker? *949*

Better it were if I'd looked for succor
Somewhere else, I would have kept my honor,
Nothing could have lured me from my affair,
I'm forced to turn tail in rout and dishonor, *953*
Help me, help me, both the bigger and smaller!
What? Without landing a blow I surrender?
Or will Pity, going along with this prayer,
Cure a poor wretch without making him sicker? *957*

Vng temps viendra qui fera dessechier,
Jaunir, flestrir vostre espanye fleur,
Je m'en risse se tant peusse maschier
Lors, mais nennil, ce seroit donc foleur,
Viel je seray, vous, laide, sans couleur,
Or beuvez fort tant que ru peut courir,
Ne donnez pas a tous ceste douleur,
Sans empirer ung povre secourir.

Prince amoureux, des amans le greigneur,
Vostre mal gré ne vouldroye encourir
Mais tout franc cuer doit par Nostre Seigneur
Sans empirer ung povre secourir.

Item, a maistre Ythier Marchant
Auquel mon branc laissai jadis
Donne, mais qu'il le mette en chant,
Ce lay contenant des vers dix
Et au luz ung *De profundis*
Pour ses ancïennes amours
Desquelles le nom je ne dis
Car il me hairoit a tous jours.

LAY

Mort, j'appelle de ta rigueur
Qui m'as ma maistresse ravie
Et n'es pas encore assouvie
Se tu ne me tiens en langueur,
Oncques puis n'euz force, vigueur,
Mais que te nuysoit elle en vie?
Mort.

Deux estions et n'avions qu'ung cuer,
S'il est mort, force est que devie,
Voire, ou que je vive sans vie
Comme les images, par cuer,
Mort.

A time is coming that will wither,
Yellow and wilt your blossoming flower,
I'll laugh, if my mouth will open that far
Then, but no, it would only look queer, *961*
I will be old, you, ugly, drained of color,
Then drink up while still flows the river,
And don't drive everyone to this despair,
Cure a poor wretch without making him sicker. *965*

Amorous prince and supreme lover,
I don't want to incur disfavor
But every free heart should for Our Seigneur
Cure a poor wretch without making him sicker. *969*

Item, to Master Ythier Marchant
To whom I once before gave my cutlass
I give, provided he sets it to music,
This lay made up of ten verses
And a *De profundis* for the lute
For all his former mistresses
Whose names I won't give out
For he would hate me forever after.

LAY

Death, I appeal your rigor
You have robbed me of my mistress
And still you remain unsatisfied
Unless you see me languish too,
Since then I've had no strength or power,
But in life what did she do to you?
Death. *984*

We were two, we shared one heart,
If it is dead then I must die as well,
Yes, or else live without life
As likenesses do, by heart,
Death. *989*

Item, a maistre Jehan Cornu
Autre nouveau laiz lui vueil faire
Car il m'a tous jours secouru
A mon grant besoing et affaire:
Pour ce le jardin luy transfere
Que maistre Pierre Bobignon
M'arenta, en faisant refaire
L'uys et redrecier le pignon.

Par faulte d'ung uys j'y perdis
Ung grez et ung manche de houe,
Alors huit faulcons non pas dix
N'y eussent pas prins une aloue:
L'ostel est seur mais qu'on le cloue,
Pour enseigne y mis ung havet,
Qui que l'ait prins, point ne m'en loue,
Sanglante nuyt et bas chevet!

Item, et pour ce que la femme
De maistre Pierre Saint Amant
(Combien, se coulpe y a a l'ame,
Dieu luy pardonne doulcement)
Me mist ou renc de cayement,
Pour *le Cheval Blanc* qui ne bouge
Luy change a une jument
Et *la Mulle* a ung asne rouge.

Item, donne a sire Denis
Hesselin, esleu de Paris,
Quatorze muys de vin d'Aulnis
Prins sur Turgis a mes perilz:
S'il en buvoit tant que peris
En fust son sens et sa raison
Qu'on mette de l'eaue es barilz,
Vin pert mainte bonne maison.

Item, to Master Jean Cornu
I would make an additional legacy
Because he always helped me out
In my worst needs and affairs, 993
And so I give him the garden
That Master Pierre Bobignon
Rented me, in getting repaired
The door and erecting the gable again. 997

For lack of a door I lost there
A hone and the shaft of a mattock,
Back then eight falcons and not ten
Couldn't have caught a lark inside, 1001
The house is safe if it's banged shut,
As a house-sign I hung up a grub-hoe,
Whoever stole it thank me not,
A bloody night and a low pillow! 1005

Item, and because the wife
Of Master Pierre Saint-Amant
(And if there be guilt in her soul,
May God absolve her in His grace) 1009
Treated me just like a beggar,
For *The White Horse* that doesn't budge
I give him in exchange a mare,
For *The She-Mule* a red-hot ass. 1013

Item, I give to Sire Denis
Hesselin elect of Paris,
Fourteen barrels of Aulnis wine
Stolen from Turgis at my peril: 1017
If he drinks enough of it to kill
His good sense and his reason
Then put water in the barrels,
Wine wrecks many a happy home. 1021

Item, donne a mon advocat
Maistre Guillaume Charruau,
Quoy que Marchant ot pour estat,
Mon branc, je me tais du fourreau,
Il aura avec ce ung reau
En change affin que sa bource enfle
Prins sur la chaussee et carreau
De la grant cousture du Temple.

Item, mon procureur Fournier
Aura pour toutes ses corvees
(Simple sera de l'espargnier)
En ma bource quatre havees
Car maintes causes m'a sauvees,
Justes, ainsi Jhesu Christ m'aide,
Comme telles se sont trouvees,
Mais bon droit a bon mestier d'aide.

Item, je donne a maistre Jaques
Raguier *le Grant Godet* de Greve
Pourveu qu'il paiera quatre plaques
Deust il vendre, quoy qu'il luy griefve,
Ce dont on cueuvre mol et greve,
Aller sans chausses, en eschappin
Se sans moy boit, assiet ne lieve,
Au trou de *la Pomme de Pin.*

Item, quant est de Merebeuf
Et de Nicolas de Louviers,
Vache ne leur donne ne beuf
Car vachiers ne sont ne bouviers
Mais gens a porter espreviers
(Ne cuidez pas que je me joue)
Et pour prendre perdris, plouviers
San faillir, sur la Machecoue.

Item, I give to my lawyer
Master Guillaume Charruau,
Whatever Marchant got to set him up,
My cutlass, I shut up about the sheath, *1025*
Along with this he'll get a *reau*
In small change to swell his purse
Picked up on the pavement and square
Of the Templars' big country place. *1029*

Item, Fournier my solicitor
Shall receive for all his bother
(It will be easy to spare him)
Four free samples out of my purse *1033*
For winning me so many cases,
Just ones, so help me Jesus Christ,
This is the way they were proved,
But the best cause needs the best lawyer. *1037*

Item, I give to Master Jacques
Raguier *The Big Wine Cup* at Grève
Provided that he pays four *plaques*
Even must he sell to his pain *1041*
That which lays on calf and shin
And go bare-legged, in little pumps
If he drinks, sits, or rises without me
At the dive *The Pine Cone.* *1045*

Item, as for Merebeuf
And Nicolas de Louviers,
I leave them neither cow nor ox
For they aren't cowherds or beefeaters *1049*
But men for carrying falcons
(Don't think I'm being humorous)
And picking up quail and plover
Without a miss, at Machecoue's. *1053*

Item, viengne Robin Turgis
A moy, je luy paieray son vin,
Combien s'il treuve mon logis
Plus fort sera que le devin:
Le droit luy donne d'eschevin
Que j'ay comme enfant de Paris,
Se je parle ung peu poictevin
Ice m'ont deux dames apris.

Elles sont tres belles et gentes
Demourans a Saint Generou
Pres Saint Julien de Voventes,
Marche de Bretaigne ou Poictou,
Mais i ne di proprement ou
Yquelles passent tous les jours,
M'arme, i ne seu mie si fou,
Car i vueil celer mes amours.

Item, a Jehan Raguier je donne,
Qui est sergent, voire des Douze,
Tant qu'il vivra, ainsi l'ordonne,
Tous les jours une tallemouse
Pour bouter et fourrer sa mouse
Prinse a la table de Bailly,
A Maubué sa gorge arrouse
Car au mengier n'a pas failly.

Item, et au Prince des Sotz
Pour ung bon sot Michault du Four
Qui a la fois dit de bons motz
Et chante bien "Ma doulce amour!"
Je lui donne avec le bonjour,
Brief, mais qu'il fust ung peu en point
Il est ung droit sot de sejour
Et est plaisant ou il n'est point.

Item, if Robin Turgis comes
To visit me, I'll pay him for his wine,
However, if he finds my room
He's cleverer than a clairvoyant: *1057*
I give him the right of alderman
I have from being Paris-born,
The reason I speak in Poitevin
Is that I was taught it by two women. *1061*

They're very beautiful and kind
And live at Saint-Géneroux
Near Saint-Julien de Voventes,
Province of Bretaigne or Poitou, *1065*
But I'm not saying where exactly
They hang out during the day,
By my soul, I'm not that crazy,
I like to keep my loves tucked away. *1069*

Item, I give to Jean Raguier,
Who is sergeant, no less, of the Twelve,
I order that he get, for life,
A great big *tallemousse* every day *1073*
In which to poke and stuff his face
Taken from the table at Bailly's
And afterward the Maubué to rinse his throat
For at eating he has never failed. *1077*

Item, to the Prince of Fools
A loyal fool Michault du Four
Who can both coin a witty phrase
And nicely sing "Ma Douce Amour!" 1081
I give him along with a *bonjour,*
Anyway, if brushed up a bit,
He's a true fool when he's there
And a funny one when he's not. *1085*

Item, aux Unze Vingtz Sergens
Donne, car leur fait est honneste
Et sont bonnes et doulces gens,
Denis Richier et Jehan Vallette,
A chascun une grant cornete
Pour pendre a leurs chappeaulx de faultres,
J'entens a ceulx a pié, hohete,
Car je n'ay que faire des autres.

De rechief donne a Perrenet,
J'entens le Bastart de la Barre,
Pour ce qu'il est beau filz et net
En son escu en lieu de barre
Trois dez plombez de bonne carre
Et ung beau joly jeu de cartes,
Mais quoy? s'on l'oyt vecir ne poirre
En oultre aura les fievres quartes.

Item, ne vueil plus que Cholet
Dolle, tranche, douve ne boise,
Relie broc ne tonnelet,
Mais tous ses houstilz changier voise
A une espee lyonnoise
Et retiengne le hutinet,
Combien qu'il n'ayme bruyt ne noise
Si luy plaist il ung tantinet.

Item, je donne a Jehan le Lou,
Homme de bien et bon marchant,
Pour ce qu'il est linget et flou
Et que Cholet est mal serchant
Ung beau petit chiennet couchant
Qui ne laira poullaille en voye,
Le long tabart est bien cachant
Pour les mussier, qu'on ne les voye.

Item, to the sergeants of the Two-twenty
I give, because their job is straight
And they are upright and courteous gents,
Denis Richier and Jean Vallette, *1089*
A very long cornet apiece
For letting dangle from their felt hats,
I mean the foot patrol, of course,
The other kind I haven't met. *1093*

Again, I give to Perrenet,
I mean the Bastard of the Bar,
Because he's a fine lad, cleancut,
On his escutcheon instead of the bar *1097*
Three loaded dice carefully squared
And a prettied-up deck of cards,
But wait, if he's caught farting silently or aloud
May he get the ague besides. *1101*

Item, I wish Cholet no longer
To adze, carve, stave, and assemble
And band up firkins and barrels,
But to trade in all his tools *1105*
For a single sword from Lyon
And just keep his little cooper's mallet,
Much as he dislikes knocking and banging
Yet he does enjoy it just a bit. *1109*

Item, I give to Jean le Lou,
Man of parts and smart merchant,
Seeing how he's delicate and frail
And Cholet's no good at the hunt, *1113*
A fine little puppy pointer
Who won't let a chick get away,
The long tabard has lots of room
For sticking them in, where none can see. *1117*

Item, a l'Orfevre de Bois
Donne cent clouz, queues et testes,
De gingembre sarrazinois
Non pas pour accomplir ses boites
Mais pour conjoindre culz et coetes
Et couldre jambons et andoulles
Tant que le lait en monte aux tetes
Et le sang en devalle aux coulles.

Au cappitaine Jehan Riou,
Tant pour luy que pour ses archiers,
Je donne six hures de lou
Qui n'est pas vïande a porchiers,
Prinses a gros mastins de bouchiers
Et cuites en vin de buffet,
Pour mengier de ces morceaulx chiers
On en feroit bien ung malfait.

C'est vïande ung peu plus pesante
Que duvet n'est, plume, ne liege,
Elle est bonne a porter en tente
Ou pour user en quelque siege,
S'ilz estoient prins a un piege,
Que ces mastins ne sceussent courre,
J'ordonne, moy qui suis son miege,
Que des peaulx, sur l'iver, se fourre.

Item, a Robinet Trascaille
Qui en service (c'est bien fait)
A pié ne va comme une caille
Mais sur roncin gras et reffait,
Je lui donne de mon buffet
Une jatte qu'emprunter n'ose
Si aura mesnage parfait,
Plus ne luy failloit autre chose.

Item, I give The Woodworker
A hundred spikes, both tails and heads,
Of ginger from the Saracens
Not for finishing his boxes *1121*
But for conjoining pussies to pricks
And sewing hams to sausages
So that milk rises to the teats
And blood rushes down to the balls. *1125*

To Captain Jean Riou,
For him and also for his archers,
I give a half-dozen heads of wolves
Which is meat not fit for swineherds, *1129*
Snatched from the butchers' big mastiffs
And cooked up in turned wine,
To taste of these gourmet's gobbets
A fellow would gladly commit a crime. *1133*

It's a meat a bit heavier
Than eiderdown, feathers, or cork,
It's excellent for encampments
Or for use while under siege, *1137*
If they were caught by means of snares.
And these dogs are poor hunters
I order him, as I'm his doctor,
This winter to use their skins for furs. *1141*

Item, to Robinet Trascaille
Who on the job (he's good at it)
Doesn't go on foot like a quail
But rides a fat and hefty mount, *1145*
I give him from my kitchen shelf
A dish he was afraid to borrow,
Thus his ménage will be complete,
He had need of nothing else. *1149*

Item, donne a Perrot Girart,
Barbier juré du Bourg la Royne,
Deux bacins et ung coquemart
Puis qu'a gaignier met telle paine:
Des ans y a demie douzaine
Qu'en son hostel de cochons gras
M'apatella une sepmaine,
Tesmoing l'abesse de Pourras.

Item, aux Freres mendians,
Aux Devotes et aux Beguines,
Tant de Paris que d'Orleans,
Tant Turlupins que Turlupines,
De grasses souppes jacoppines
Et flans leur fais oblacion
Et puis après soubz ces courtines
Parler de contemplacion.

Si ne suis je pas qui leur donne
Mais de tous enffans sont les meres
Et Dieu, qui ainsi les guerdonne,
Pour qui seuffrent paines ameres:
Il faut qu'ilz vivent, les beaulx peres,
Et mesmement ceulx de Paris,
S'ilz font plaisir a nos commeres
Ilz ayment ainsi leurs maris.

Quoy que maistre Jehan de Poullieu
En voulsist dire *et reliqua*
Contraint et en publique lieu
Honteusement s'en revoqua:
Maistre Jehan de Mehun s'en moqua
De leur façon, si fist Mathieu,
Mais on doit honnorer ce qu'a
Honnoré l'Eglise de Dieu.

Item, I give to Perrot Girart,
Sworn barber of Bourg-la-Reine,
Two bowls and a big-bellied pot
Since he slaves to make ends meet: *1153*
It was a half dozen years back
That on succulent pig, in his own house,
He forcefed me a whole week,
Witness the Abbess of Pourras. *1157*

Item, to the Mendicant Friars,
The Devotes and the Beguines
Of Paris as well as Orléans,
Turlupins as well as Turlupines, *1161*
With the Jacobins' rich soups
And custards I make them an oblation
And afterward behind bed curtains
Discussions about contemplation. *1165*

It's not me who makes them gifts,
It's the mother of every child
And God, who gives them this reward,
For whom they have to go through hell: *1169*
They've got to live, these handsome fathers,
Just as do the ones in Paris,
If they give some goodwife pleasure
They thus show their love for her spouse. *1173*

Whatever Master Jean de Poullieu
Wished to say on this *et reliqua*
Under constraint and in public
Humiliated he took it back: *1177*
Master Jean de Meung satirized
Their ways, and Matheolus also did,
But one must honor that which is
Honored by the Church of God. *1181*

Si me soubmectz, leur serviteur,
En tout ce que puis faire et dire
A les honnorer de bon cuer
Et obeïr sans contredire:
L'homme bien fol est d'en mesdire
Car soit a part ou en preschier
Ou ailleurs il ne fault pas dire,
Ses gens sont pour eux revenchier.

Item, je donne a frere Baude
Demourant en l'ostel des Carmes,
Portant chiere hardie et baude,
Une sallade et deux guysarmes
Que Detusca et ses gens d'armes
Ne lui riblent sa caige vert,
Viel est, s'il ne se rent aux armes
C'est bien le deable de Vauvert.

Item, pour ce que le Scelleur
Maint estront de mouche a maschié
Donne, car homme est de valeur,
Son seau d'avantage crachié
Et qu'il ait le poulce escachié
Pour tout empreindre a une voye,
J'entens celuy de l'Eveschié
Car les autres, Dieu les pourvoye.

Quant des auditeurs messeigneurs
Leur granche ilz auront lambroissee
Et ceulx qui ont les culz rongneux
Chascun une chaire percee
Mais qu'a la petite Macee
D'Orleans, qui ot ma sainture,
L'amende soit bien hault tauxee,
Elle est une mauvaise ordure.

And so, their servant, I accept
In everything I do or say
To honor them with all my heart
And submit unquestioningly: *1185*
Whoever attacks them is a fool
For in private or on the podium
Or wherever, you should keep still,
These people can strike back. *1189*

Item, I give to Friar Baude
Who lives in the house for Carmelites
And seems very brave and bold
A helmet and a pair of pikes *1193*
To keep De Tusca and his armed men
From messing around in his love nest,
He's old, if he doesn't lay down his weapon
He's surely the Devil of Vauvert. *1197*

Item, because the Keeper of the Seal
Has eaten plenty of beeshit
I give, as he's a man of honor,
His seal with spit already on it *1201*
And may he have his thumb squashed flat
For stamping all with a single thrust,
I mean the one the Bishop's got
Because God provides for the rest. *1205*

As for milords the auditors
Wainscot paneling for their barn
And to each of them whose ass is sore
I bequeath a pierced potty-chair *1209*
Provided that for little Macée
Of Orléans, who got my belt,
They jack the fine up good and high,
She is a smelly piece of filth. *1213*

Item, donne a maistre Françoys,
Promoteur, de la Vacquerie,
Ung hault gorgerin d'Escossoys
Toutesfois sans orfaverie
Car quant receut chevallerie
Il maugrea Dieu et saint George,
Parler n'en oit qui ne s'en rie
Comme enragié, a plaine gorge.

Item, a maistre Jehan Laurens
Qui a les povres yeulx si rouges
Pour le pechié de ses parens
Qui boivent en barilz et courges
Je donne l'envers de mes bouges
Pour tous les matins les torchier,
S'il fust arcevesque de Bourges
Du sendail eust, mais il est chier.

Item, a maistre Jehan Cotart,
Mon procureur en court d'Eglise,
Devoye environ ung patart,
Car a present bien m'en advise,
Quant chicaner me feist Denise
Disant que l'avoye mauldite,
Pour son ame, qu'es cieulx soit mise,
Ceste oroison j'ai cy escripte.

BALLADE

Pere Noé qui plantastes la vigne,
Vous aussi, Loth, qui beustes ou rochier
Par tel party qu'Amours, qui gens engigne,
De voz filles si vous feist approuchier
(Pas ne le dy pour le vous reprouchier)
Archetriclin, qui bien sceustes cest art,
Tous trois vous pry que vous vueillez peschier
L'ame du bon feu maistre Jehan Cotart.

Item, I give to Master François,
Promoter, from La Vacquerie,
A close-fitting Scottish gorget
Plain without embroidery 1217
Because when he was dubbed a knight
He cursed, "By God and by Saint George,"
All who hear the tale burst out
Laughing like mad, with belly laughs. 1221

Item, to Master Jean Laurens
Whose poor little eyes are all red
Thanks to the sins of his parents
Who drank by the pailful and keg 1225
I give the linings of my money bags
For wiping them out with every day,
If he were archbishop of Bourges
I'd give him silk, but it runs high. 1229

Item, to Master Jean Cotart,
My solicitor in the Court of Church,
I owed approximately one *patart,*
I only realized it now, 1233
From the time Denise had me pulled in
On the complaint that I'd abused her,
To help his soul get into heaven
I've written the following prayer. 1237

BALLADE

Father Noah who planted the vine
And you too, Lot, who swilled in the cave
In such a way that Love, who outwits people,
Had you coupled with your own daughters 1241
(I don't say this to blame you for it)
And Architriclinus, who well knew the art,
All three of you I pray please fish out
The soul of the late good Master Jean Cotart. 1245

Jadis extraict il fut de vostre ligne,
Luy qui buvoit du meilleur et plus chier
Et ne deust il avoir vaillant ung pigne,
Certes, sur tous, c'estoit ung bon archier,
On ne luy sceut pot des mains arrachier,
De bien boire ne fut oncques fetart,
Nobles seigneurs, ne souffrez empeschier
L'ame du bon feu maistre Jehan Cotart.

Comme homme beu qui chancelle et trepigne
L'ay veu souvent quant il s'alloit couchier
Et une fois il se feist une bigne,
Bien m'en souvient, a l'estal d'ung bouchier:
Brief, on n'eust sceu en ce monde serchier
Meilleur pyon pour boire tost et tart,
Faictes entrer quant vous orrez huchier
L'ame du bon feu maistre Jehan Cotart.

Prince, il n'eust sceu jusqu'a terre crachier,
Tousjours crioit, "Haro! la gorge m'art!"
Et si ne sceust oncq sa seuf estanchier
L'ame du bon feu maistre Jehan Cotart.

Item, vueil que le jeune Merle
Desormais gouverne mon change
Car de changier envys me mesle,
Pourveu que tousjours baille en change
Soit a privé soit a estrange
Pour trois escus six brettes targes,
Pour deux angelotz ung grant ange,
Car amans doivent estre larges.

Item, j'ay sceu en ce voyage
Que mes trois povres orphelins
Sont creus et deviennent en aage
Et n'ont pas testes de belins
Et qu'enfans d'icy a Salins
N'a mieulx sachans leur tour d'escolle,
Or par l'ordre des Mathelins
Telle jeunesse n'est pas folle.

He was of your lineage in former days,
He who drank only the best and highest priced
Even when he couldn't raise the price of a comb,
He was the first of tosspots, *1249*
You couldn't tear the winejug from his grip,
He was never slow to drink deep,
Noble lords, don't let anything hold up
The soul of the late good Master Jean Cotart. *1253*

Like some old drunk who staggers and reels
I've often seen him going home to bed
And once he raised himself a big welt,
I remember it well, on a butcher stall: *1257*
In short, you couldn't have found this world over
A better souse for drinking day and night,
Have him come in when you hear sing out
The soul of the late good Master Jean Cotart. *1261*

Prince, he couldn't have spit as far as his feet,
He was always crying, "Fire! Fire in the throat!"
And so he could never appease his thirst
The soul of the late good Master Jean Cotart. *1265*

Item, I will that the young Merle
Henceforth look after my money-changing
For I do it against my will,
On condition that he always exchange *1269*
Whether to friend or to stranger
For three *écus* six Breton *targes,*
For two angelets a big angel,
Because lovers ought to fork out. *1273*

Item, I learned during my trip
That my three poor little orphans
Have grown up and come of age
And are far from being morons *1277*
And that no children from here to Salins
Are better at their lessons,
Now by the Order of Mathurins
Such a childhood isn't misspent. *1281*

Si vueil qu'ilz voisent a l'estude,
Ou? sur maistre Pierre Richier,
Le Donat est pour eulx trop rude,
Ja ne les y vueil empeschier,
Ilz sauront, je l'ayme plus chier,
Ave salus, tibi decus
Sans plus grans lettres enserchier,
Tousjours n'ont pas clers l'au dessus.

Cecy estudient, et ho,
Plus proceder je leur deffens,
Quant d'entendre le grant *Credo*
Trop forte elle est pour telz enfans:
Mon long tabart en deux je fens,
Si vueil que la moitié s'en vende
Pour eulx en acheter des flans
Car jeunesse est ung peu friande.

Et vueil qu'ilz soient informez
En meurs, quoy que couste bature,
Chaperons auront enformez
Et les poulces sur la sainture,
Humbles a toute creature,
Disans, "Han? Quoy? Il n'en est rien,"
Si diront gens, par adventure,
"Vecy enfans de lieu de bien."

Item, et mes povres clerjons
Auxquelz mes tiltres resigné,
Beaulx enfans et droiz comme jons,
Les voyant m'en dessaisiné
Cens recevoir leur assigné
(Seur comme qui l'auroit en paulme
A ung certain jour consigné)
Sur l'ostel de Gueuldry Guillaume.

So I'd like them to get educated,
Where? At Master Pierre Richier's,
The Donatus is too hard for them
And I don't want anything holding them back, *1285*
I'd much prefer that they pick up
Ave salus, tibi decus
Without delving into higher matters,
Scholars don't always come out on top. *1289*

Let them study this far, then whoa,
I forbid them to go any farther,
As for getting into the great Credo
It's too potent for these youngsters: *1293*
I rip my long tabard in two,
One half is to be put on sale
To buy for them some custard pie
For young fellows have a sweet tooth. *1297*

And I wish them to be given lessons
In manners, cost what it may in thrashings,
They'll wear close-fitting chaperons
And hook their thumbs in their sashes, *1301*
Playing humble to everybody,
Saying, "Huh? What? Aw, it's nothing,"
So that people will remark, maybe,
"There go children from a nice family." *1305*

Item, to my poor little clerks
To whom I signed over my titles,
Fine boys, erect as bulrushes,
One look at them and I renounced *1309*
And assigned to them the back rent
(As good as in the hand already
Consigned on such and such a day)
On the house of Guillaume Gueuldry. *1313*

Quoy que jeunes et esbatans
Soient, en riens ne me desplaist,
Dedens trente ans ou quarante ans
Bien autres seront, se Dieu plaist:
Il fait mal qui ne leur complaist,
Ilz sont tres beaulx enfans et gens
Et qui les bat ne fiert fol est
Car enfans si deviennent gens.

Les bources des Dix et Huit Clers
Auront, je m'y vueil travaillier,
Pas ilz ne dorment comme loirs
Qui trois mois sont sans resveillier,
Au fort, triste est le sommeillier
Qui fait aisier jeune en jeunesse
Tant qu'en fin lui faille veillier
Quant reposer deust en viellesse.

Si en rescrips au collateur
Lettres semblables et pareilles,
Or prient pour leur bienfaicteur
Ou qu'on leur tire les oreilles:
Aucunes gens ont grans merveilles
Que tant m'encline vers ces deux
Mais, foy que doy festes et veilles,
Oncques ne vy les meres d'eulx.

Item, donne a Michault Cul d'Oue
Et a sire Charlot Taranne
Cent solz (s'ilz demandent, "Prins ou?"
Ne leur chaille, ilz vendront de manne)
Et unes houses de basanne,
Autant empeigne que semelle,
Pourveu qu'ilz me salueront Jehanne
Et autant une autre comme elle.

Although they're young and unruly
They don't displease me in the least,
Thirty or forty years from now,
God willing, they'll be something else: *1317*
One's wrong not to give them their way,
These are fine, courteous children
And whoever beats or hits them is crazy
For children grow up to be men. *1321*

The purses of the Eighteen Clerks
They'll have, I want to take some pains,
They don't sleep as the dormice do
Which sleep three months at a stretch: *1325*
In any case, the sleep's pathetic
That young fellows enjoy in youth
For at last they have to stay up
When they're old and could use a rest. *1329*

And so I'll write the collator
Matching and identical letters,
Let them pray for their benefactor
Or else may someone yank their ears: *1333*
Some people are a little shocked
That I'm so friendly toward this pair
But, by my faith in feasts and wakes,
I have never once eyed their mothers. *1337*

Item, I give to Michault Culdoe
And to Sire Charlot Taranne
A hundred *sous* (if they ask, "Got how?"
Don't worry, it'll fall like manna) *1341*
And a pair of boots in sheepskin,
The uppers as well as the soles,
Provided they give my love to Jeanne
And to one more of her calling. *1345*

Item, au seigneur de Grigny
Auquel jadis laissay Vicestre
Je donne la tour de Billy
Pourveu s'uys y a ne fenestre
Quit soit ne debout ne en estre
Qu'il mette tres bien tout a point,
Face argent a destre et senestre,
Il m'en fault et il n'en a point.

Item, a Thibault de la Garde
(Thibault? je mens, il a nom Jehan)
Que luy donray je, que ne perde?
Assez ay perdu tout cest an,
Dieu y vueille pourveoir, *amen,*
Le Barillet, par m'ame, voire,
Genevoys est plus ancïen
Et a plus beau nez pour y boire.

Item, je donne a Basennier,
Notaire et greffier criminel,
De giroffle plain ung pannier
Prins sur maistre Jehan de Ruel,
Tant a Mautaint, tant a Rosnel,
Et avec ce don de giroffle
Servir de cuer gent et ysnel
Le seigneur qui sert saint Cristofle,

Auquel ceste ballade donne
Pour sa dame, qui tous biens a,
S'amour ainsi tous ne guerdonne
Je ne m'esbays de cela
Car au pas conquester l'ala
Que tint Regnier, roy de Cecille,
Ou si bien fist et peu parla
Qu'onques Hector fist ne Troïlle.

Item, to the lord of Grigny
To whom I left Bicêtre already
I give the Tower of Billy
Providing if there's a door or window 1349
Which doesn't stand in working order
He fix it up like new again,
May he make money right and left,
I need it and he has none. 1353

Item, to Thibault de la Garde
(Thibault? I'm lying, his name is Jean)
What shall I give so as not to lose out?
I've lost enough throughout the year, 1357
May God make it up to me, amen,
The Wine Keg, by my soul, just right,
But Genevois is an older man
With a brighter nose for drinking there. 1361

Item, I give to Basanier,
Notary and criminal registrar,
A wicker basket filled with cloves
Stolen from Master Jean de Ruel, 1365
The same to Mautaint and Rosnel,
And in addition to the cloves I give
The right to serve with grace and cheer
The lord who serves Saint Christopher, 1369

To whom I offer this *ballade*
For his lady, who has every grace,
If love does not thus reward us all
I don't think it's any wonder, 1373
For he went to win her at the tourney
Held by Regnier king of Sicily
Where he fought as well and bragged as little
As ever Hector did or Troilus. 1377

BALLADE

Au poinct du jour que l'esprevier s'esbat
Meu de plaisir et par noble coustume,
Bruit la maulvis et de joye s'esbat,
Reçoit son per et se joinct a sa plume,
Offrir vous vueil, a ce desir m'alume,
Ioyeusement ce qu'aux amans bon semble,
Sachiez qu'Amour l'escript en son volume
Et c'est la fin pour quoy sommes ensemble.

Dame serez de mon cuer sans debat,
Entierement, jusques mort me consume,
Lorier souef qui pour mon droit combat,
Olivier franc m'ostant toute amertume:
Raison ne veult que je desacoustume
Et en ce vueil avec elle m'assemble,
De vous servir, mais que m'y acoustume,
Et c'est la fin pour quoy sommes ensemble.

Et qui plus est, quant dueil sur moy s'embat
Par Fortune qui souvent si se fume
Vostre doulx oeil sa malice rabat
Ne mais ne mains que le vent fait la plume:
Si ne pers pas la graine que je sume
En vostre champ quant le fruit me ressemble,
Dieu m'ordonne que le fouÿsse et fume
Et c'est la fin pour quoy sommes ensemble.

Princesse, oyez ce que cy vous resume,
Que le mien cuer du vostre desassemble
Ja ne sera, tant de vous en presume,
Et c'est la fin pour quoy sommes ensemble.

Item, a sire Jehan Perdrier
Riens, n'a Françoys son secont frere,
Si m'ont voulu tous jours aidier
Et de leurs biens faire confrere,

BALLADE

At daybreak when the sparrow-hawk disports
Sent up by delight and noble custom
And the throstle calls and flutters happily,
Receives her mate and surrenders in his plumes, *1381*
Aroused by passion I wish to offer you
Joyfully that which so appeals to lovers,
Know that Love inscribes this in her book
And this is the end for which we are together. *1385*

You shall be sole mistress of my heart,
Totally, until death has brought me low,
Gracious laurel who battles for my right,
Brave olive branch freeing me of bitterness: *1389*
Reason wishes that I keep the habit,
And in this wish I'm in accord with her,
Of serving you, and grow addicted to it,
And this is the end for which we are together. *1393*

And what's more, when sorrow assails me
Through Fortune who's often full of anger
Your calm eye deflects its malice
Just the way the breeze does the feather: *1397*
I do not lose the seed I put down here
In your field, for the harvest repeats me,
God commands I fork and fertilize it
And this is the end for which we are together. *1401*

Princess, hear what I say in summary,
May the turning away of my heart from yours
Never happen, I presume you wish the same,
And this is the end for which we are together. *1405*

Item, to Sire Jean Perdrier
Nothing, nor to François his little brother,
It's true they always helped me out
And shared and shared alike their goods, *1409*

Combien que Françoys mon compere,
Langues cuisans flambans et rouges,
My commandement, my priere,
Me recommanda fort a Bourges.

Si allé veoir en Taillevent
Ou chappitre de fricassure,
Tout au long, derriere et devant,
Lequel n'en parle jus ne sure,
Mais Macquaire, je vous asseure,
A tout le poil cuisant ung deable
Affin qu'il sentist bon l'arsure
Ce *recipe* m'escript, sans fable.

BALLADE

En realgar, en arcenic rochier,
En orpiment, en salpestre et chaulx vive,
En plomb boullant pour mieulx les esmorchier,
En suye et poix destrempez de lessive
Faicte d'estrons et de pissat de juifve,
En lavailles de jambes a meseaulx,
En racleure de piez et viels houseaulx,
En sang d'aspic et drogues venimeuses,
En fiel de loups, de regnars et blereaulx,
Soient frittes ces langues envieuses.

En cervelle de chat qui hayt peschier,
Noir, et si viel qu'il n'ait dent en gencive,
D'ung viel mastin qui vault bien aussi chier,
Tout enragié, en sa bave et salive,
En l'escume d'une mulle poussive
Detrenchiee menu a bons ciseaulx,
En eaue ou ratz plongent groings et museaulx,
Raines, crappaulx et bestes dangereuses,
Serpens, lesars et telz nobles oyseaulx,
Soient frittes ces langues envieuses.

However François my friend,
Those smarting, fiery, red-hot tongues,
Now entreating me, now bullying,
Did strongly urge on me at Bourges. *1413*

So I went and looked at Taillevent
In the chapter on how to fry,
The whole length, behind and in front,
And it isn't mentioned up or down, *1417*
But I can assure you Macquaire
Who cooks a devil in all his hair
To make him smell good while burning
Wrote me out this recipe, I swear. *1421*

BALLADE

In smoke of minerals, in arsenic,
In orpiment, saltpeter and quicklime,
In boiling lead to get them precooked,
In soot and pitch marinated in lye
Made out of the turds and piss of Jews, *1426*
In old washwater from the legs of lepers,
In items scraped off feet and shoesoles,
In poisonous drugs and in asp blood,
In wolf, fox, and polecat gall,
These envious tongues are to be fried. *1431*

In the brains of a cat who hates to fish,
A black one so old he hasn't a tooth to his gums,
Or some mangy cur worth about as much,
A mad one, in its slobber and spittle,
In the slaver of a wheezy mule *1436*
Cut up fine with sharp scissors,
In water in which rats poke snouts and muzzles,
Also frogs, toads, and dangerous animals,
Snakes, lizards and suchlike noble birds,
These envious tongues are to be fried. *1441*

En sublimé dangereux a touchier
Et ou nombril d'une couleuvre vive,
En sang qu'on voit es palletes sechier
Sur ces barbiers, quant plaine lune arrive,
Dont l'ung est noir, l'autre plus vert que cive,
En chancre et fiz et en ces ors curveaulx
Ou nourrisses essangent leurs drappeaulx,
En petiz baings de filles amoureuses
(Qui ne m'entent n'a suivy les bordeaulx)
Soient frittes ces langues envieuses.

Prince, passez tous ces frians morceaulx,
S'estamine, sacs n'avez ou bluteaulx,
Parmy le fons d'unes brayes breneuses,

Mais, par avant, en estrons de pourceaulx
Soient frittes ces langues envieuses.

Item, a maistre Andry Courault
"Les Contrediz Franc Gontier" mande,
Quant du tirant seant en hault,
A cestuy la riens ne demande:
Le Saige ne veult que contende
Contre puissant povre homme las
Affin que ses fillez ne tende
Et qu'il ne trebuche en ses las.

Gontier ne crains, il n'a nuls hommes
Et mieulx que moy n'est herité,
Mais en ce debat cy nous sommes
Car il loue sa povreté,
Estre povre yver et esté,
Et a felicité repute
Ce que tiens a maleureté,
Lequel a tort? Or en discute.

In sublimates too risky to handle,
In the navel of a snake who's still alive,
In the blood you see drying in basins
In barbershops when the moon is full,
One black, the other greener than chives, *1446*
In sores and excrescences, in the dirty vats
In which wet-nurses throw crotch-rags to soak,
In the little bidets used by professionals
(Who doesn't get me hasn't been to brothels)
These envious tongues are to be fried. *1451*

Prince, pass all these delectable tidbits,
If you haven't bolting-cloth, sack or strainer,
Through the brown-stained seat of somebody's
drawers,
However, before you do this, in pigshit
These envious tongues are to be fried. *1456*

Item, to Master André Courault
I leave "Refuting Franc Gontier,"
As for the tyrant on his throne,
I'm not addressing this to him: *1460*
The Sage doesn't want the little guy
To tangle with those who are high up
Lest snares be set out for him
And he stumble into the trap. *1464*

I'm safe with Gontier, he has no men
And no more inheritance than I,
But we fell into this argument
Because he praises his poverty, *1468*
Being poor winter and summer,
And extols as felicitous
The things I ascribe to misery,
Who's wrong? I argue as follows. *1472*

BALLADE

Sur mol duvet assis ung gras chanoine
Lez ung brasier en chambre bien natee,
A son costé gisant dame Sidoine,
Blanche, tendre, polie et attintee,
Boire ypocras a jour et a nuytee,
Rire, jouer, mignonner et baisier,
Et nu a nu pour mieulx des corps s'aisier
Les vy tous deux par ung trou de mortaise,
Lors je congneus que pour dueil appaisier
Il n'est tresor que de vivre a son aise.

Se Franc Gontier et sa compaigne Helaine
Eussent ceste doulce vie hantee
D'oignons, civotz, qui causent forte alaine,
N'aconçassent une bise tostee,
Tout leur mathon ne toute leur potee
Ne prise ung ail, je le dy sans noysier,
S'ilz se vantent couchier soubz le rosier,
Lequel vault mieulx, lict costoyé de chaise?
Qu'en dites vous? Faut il a ce musier?
Il n'est tresor que de vivre a son aise.

De gros pain bis vivent, d'orge, d'avoine,
Et boivent eaue tout au long de l'anee,
Tous les oyseaulx d'icy en Babiloine
A tel escot une seule journee
Ne me tendroient, non une matinee:
Or s'esbate, de par Dieu, Franc Gontier,
Helaine o luy, soubz le bel esglantier,
Se bien leur est, cause n'ay qu'il me poise,
Mais quoy que soit du laboureux mestier
Il n'est tresor que de vivre a son aise.

Prince, jugiez, pour tost nous accorder,
Quant est de moy, mais qu'a nul ne desplaise,
Petit enfant j'ay oÿ recorder,
Il n'est tresor que de vivre a son aise.

BALLADE

A plump canon lounging on eiderdown
Near the coals in a well-upholstered room,
Lady Sidoine stretched out beside him,
White, delectable, glistening and primped,
Drinking hypocras by day and by night, *1477*
Laughing, tickling, caressing, kissing,
Bare skin to bare skin for the body's delight
I saw the two of them through a mortise-chink,
And then I knew that for easing off grief
There's no treasure like living high. *1482*

If Franc Gontier and his mate Helen
Had acquired a taste for this easy life
Then with onions and leeks, which give bad breath,
They wouldn't garnish their black toast,
All their yogurt and vegetable pap *1487*
I don't value a garlic, no offense meant,
They're proud of sleeping under the rose tree,
Which is better, a nice bed and chair?
What do you say? Do you have to wonder?
There's no treasure like living high. *1492*

They live on rough bread of barley and oats
And drink nothing but water the year through,
But all the birds this side of Babylon
Couldn't make me stick it out one day
At such a price, no not one morning: *1497*
So let him disport, by God, Franc Gontier,
With his Helen under the pretty eglantine,
If this is what suits them it's their business,
Whatever the life at the plow is like
There's no treasure like living high. *1502*

Prince, make a judgment, so we can agree,
As for me, let no one take offense,
When I was a child I would hear them say,
There's no treasure like living high. *1506*

Item, pour ce que scet sa Bible,
Ma damoiselle de Bruyeres,
Donne preschier hors l'Evangille
A elle et a ses bachelieres
Pour retraire ces villotieres
Qui ont le bec si affillé,
Mais que ce soit hors cymetieres,
Trop bien au marchié au fillé.

BALLADE

Quoy qu'on tient belles langagieres,
Florentines, Veniciennes,
Assez pour estre messagieres
Et mesmement les ancïennes,
Mais soient Lombardes, Rommaines,
Genevoises, a mes perilz,
Pimontoises, Savoisiennes,
Il n'est bon bec que de Paris.

De tres beau parler tiennent chaieres,
Ce dit on Neapolitaines
Et sont tres bonnes caquetieres,
Allemandes et Pruciennes,
Soient Grecques, Egipciennes,
De Hongrie ou d'autre pays,
Espaignolles ou Cathelennes,
Il n'est bon bec que de Paris.

Brette Suysses n'y sçavent guieres,
Gasconnes n'aussi Toulousaines,
De Petit Pont deux harengieres
Les concluront, et les Lorraines,
Engloises et Calaisiennes
(Ay je beaucoup de lieux compris?)
Picardes de Valenciennes,
Il n'est bon bec que de Paris.

Item, since she knows her Bible,
My Mademoiselle de Bruyères,
I leave her to preach without Gospel,
Her and all her graduate girls, 1510
To reform the streetwalkers
Who have such stinging tongues,
But let them keep out of the cemeteries,
Best of all at the dry-goods stalls. 1514

BALLADE

However famous for their talk
Are Florentine and Venetian women,
Skilled enough to be go-betweens
Even the very ancient ones, 1518
Yet be they Lombards or Romans,
Or Genovese, I'll lay you odds,
Or Piedmontese or Savoisiennes,
There's no good tongue but in Paris. 1522

In talking well they hold chairs,
The Neapolitans maintain,
And they are lively jabberers,
The Germans and the Prussians, 1526
Be they Greek or Egyptian,
Hungarian or something else,
Spanish or Catalonian,
There's no good tongue but in Paris. 1530

Bretons and Swiss don't know how,
And Gascon and Toulousian women,
Two fishwives on the Petit-Pont
Could shut them up, also the Lorraines 1534
And the English and Calaisiennes
(Haven't I touched a lot of places?)
And Picard women of Valence,
There's no good tongue but in Paris. 1538

Prince, aux dames Parisiennes
De beau parler donnez le pris,
Quoy qu'on die d'Italiennes
Il n'est bon bec que de Paris.

Regards m'en deux, trois, assises
Sur le bas du ply de leurs robes
En ces moustiers, en ces eglises,
Tire toy pres et ne te hobes,
Tu trouveras la que Macrobes
Oncques ne fist tels jugemens,
Entens, quelque chose en desrobes,
Ce sont tous beaulx enseignemens.

Item, et au mont de Montmartre
Qui est ung lieu moult ancïen
Je luy donne et adjoings le tertre
Qu'on dit le mont Valerien
Et, oultre plus, ung quartier d'an
Du pardon qu'apportay de Romme,
Si ira maint bon crestien
En l'abbaye ou il n'entre homme.

Item, varletz et chamberieres
De bons hostelz (riens ne me nuyt)
Feront tartes, flans et goyeres
Et grans ralias a myenuit
(Riens n'y font sept pintes ne huit)
Tant que gisent seigneur et dame,
Puis après, sans mener grant bruit,
Je leur ramentoy le jeu d'asne.

Item, et a filles de bien
Qui ont peres, meres et antes,
Par m'ame, je ne donne rien
Car j'ay tout donné aux servantes:
Si fussent ilz de peu contentes
Grant bien leur fissent mains loppins
Aux povres filles, entrementes
Qu'ilz se perdent aux Jacoppins,

Prince, to the Parisian women
Give the prize for talking best,
Say what you will of Italians
There's no good tongue but in Paris. *1542*

See them squatting by twos and threes
On the folded hems of their dresses
In churches and monasteries,
Steal up close without a noise, *1546*
You'll overhear such opinions
As Macrobius never dreamed of,
Pay attention and pick up some pearl,
This is a liberal education. *1550*

Item, to the Montmartre mound
Which is a very ancient site
I give and attach the rise
That's known as Mount Valerian *1554*
And I also give a quarter year
Of the indulgence I'll bring back from Rome,
Thus many a good Christian will get in
The abbey where no man enters. *1558*

Item, grooms and chambermaids
Of good households (nothing's too much for me)
Shall make tarts, custards, cheese delight
And throw big parties at midnight *1562*
(Seven, eight pints is just a start)
While lord and lady are abed,
Then, afterward, keeping down the noise,
I'll give them a refresher course in assing. *1566*

Item, and to the respectable girls
Who have father, mother and aunts,
By my soul, I can't give a thing
For I've given it all to the servants: *1570*
Although they make do with little
Some big morsels would be a boon
To the poor girls, items which meanwhile
Waste away at the Jacobins, *1574*

Aux Celestins et aux Chartreux,
Quoy que vie mainent estroite
Si ont ilz largement entre eulx
Dont povres filles ont souffrete,
Tesmoing Jaqueline, et Perrete,
Et Ysabeau qui dit, "Enné!"
Puis qu'ilz en ont telle disette
A paine en seroit on damné.

Item, a la Grosse Margot,
Tres doulce face et pourtraicture,
Foy que doy, *brulare bigod,*
Assez devote creature:
Je l'aime de propre nature
Et elle moy, la doulce sade,
Qui la trouvera d'aventure
Qu'on luy lise ceste ballade.

BALLADE

Se j'ayme et sers la belle de bon hait
M'en devez vous tenir ne vil ne sot?
Elle a en soy des biens a fin souhait,
Pour son amour sains bouclier et passot,
Quant viennent gens je cours et happe ung pot,
Au vin m'en fuis sans demener grant bruit,
Je leur tens eaue, frommage, pain et fruit,
S'ilz paient bien je leur dis, *"Bene stat,*
Retournez cy quant vous serez en ruit,
En ce bordeau ou tenons nostre estat."

Mais adoncques il y a grant deshait
Quant sans argent s'en vient couchier Margot,
Veoir ne la puis, mon cuer a mort la hait,
Sa robe prens, demy saint et surcot,
Si luy jure qu'il tendra pour l'escot,

At the Celestines and Carthusians,
Although they lead the narrow life
Between them have a large provision
Of what these girls are starving for, *1578*
Just ask Jacqueline or Perrette
Or Isabelle who comments, "Great!"
Seeing they're in such a state
You probably won't go to Hell for it. *1582*

Item, and to Fat Margot,
Very sweet in face and figure,
By the faith I owe, by heaven,
A most pious creature: *1586*
I love her for herself alone
And she me, this dainty morsel,
Whoever meets her on his rounds
Will he please read her this *ballade:* *1590*

BALLADE

If I love my fair and serve her gladly
Must I be taken for a wretch or fool?
She has graces for the subtlest desires,
For her I gird on shield and dagger,
When company comes I run and grab a pot, *1595*
Hurry for the wine careful to be quiet,
I offer them water, cheese, bread and fruit,
If they pay well I tell them, "*Bene stat,*
Drop in again the next time you feel horny,
In this whorehouse where we hold our state." *1600*

But then there's real ill-will
When Margot comes to bed without a cent,
I can't look at her, I loathe her in my heart,
I snatch her dress, the waistband and skirt,
And swear to her it will serve as my cut, *1605*

Par les costés se prent, "c'est Antecrist!"
Crie et jure par la mort Jhesucrist
Que non fera, lors j'empoingne ung esclat,
Dessus son nez luy en fais ung escript
En ce bordeau ou tenons nostre estat.

Puis paix se fait et me fait ung gros pet
Plus enflee qu'ung vlimeux escharbot,
Riant, m'assiet son poing sur mon sommet,
"Gogo," me dit et me fiert le jambot,
Tous deux yvres dormons comme ung sabot
Et au resveil quant le ventre luy bruit
Monte sur moy que ne gaste son fruit,
Soubz elle geins, plus qu'un aiz me fait plat,
De paillarder tout elle me destruit
En ce bordeau ou tenons nostre estat.

Vente, gresle, gelle, j'ay mon pain cuit,
Ie suis paillart, la paillarde me suit,
Lequel vault mieulx? Chascun bien s'entresuit
L'ung vault l'autre, c'est a mau rat mau chat,
Ordure amons, oıdure nous assuit,
Nous deffuyons onneur, il nous deffuit
En ce bordeau ou tenons nostre estat.

Item, a Marion l'Idolle
Et la grant Jehanne de Bretaigne
Donne tenir publique escolle
Ou l'escollier le maistre enseigne:
Lieu n'est ou ce marchié ne tiengne
Si non a la grisle de Mehun
De quoy je dis, "Fy de l'enseigne
Puis que l'ouvraige est si commun."

Item, et a Noel Jolis
Autre chose je ne luy donne
Fors plain poing d'osiers frez cueillis
En mon jardin, je l'abandonne,

She sticks her hands on her hips, "Anti-Christ!"
She screams and swears by the death of Jesus Christ
She won't have it. At which I pick up a slat,
Across her nose I beat it in writing
In this whorehouse where we hold our state. *1610*

Then we make peace and she lets me a big fart
Puffed up worse than a poisonous dung-beetle,
Laughing, she sits her fist on my crown,
"Baby," she says and whacks my tail,
The two of us dead drunk we sleep like a top *1615*
And when we wake and her belly cries
She climbs aboard so as not to spoil her fruit,
I groan underneath, pressed flatter than a plank,
As she wipes out all the lechery in me
In this whorehouse where we hold our state. *1620*

When it hails, blows, freezes, my bread's baked,
I'm a lecher, she's a lecher to suit,
Which one is better? We're a good pair, *1623*
One's worth the other, bad rat bad cat,
We go for filth and filth is our lot,
From honor we run and honor runs from us
In this whorehouse where we hold our state. *1627*

Item, to Marion the Idol
And Big Jeanne of Bretagne
The right to run a public school
In which the pupil drills the teacher: *1631*
This is the arrangement everywhere
Except at Meung behind bars
Which is why I say, "To hell with signs
Seeing the work is so popular." *1635*

Item, and to Noël Jolis
I don't make any gift besides
A fistful of willows freshly picked
From my garden, I cut him off, *1639*

Chastoy est une belle aulmosne,
Ame n'en doit estre marry,
Unze vings coups luy en ordonne
Livrez par les mains de Henry.

Item, ne scay qu'a l'Ostel Dieu
Donner, n'a povres hospitaulx,
Bourdes n'ont icy temps ne lieu
Car povres gens ont assez maulx,
Chascun leur envoye leurs aulx,
Les Mendians ont eu mon oye,
Au fort, ilz en auront les os,
A menue gent menue monnoye.

Item, je donne a mon barbier
Qui se nomme Colin Galerne,
Pres voisin d'Angelot l'erbier,
Ung gros glasson (prins ou? en Marne):
Affin qu'a son ayse s'yverne,
De l'estomac le tiengne pres,
Se l'yver ainsi se gouverne
Trop n'aura chault l'esté d'après.

Item, riens aux Enfans Trouvez
Mais les perdus faut que consolle,
Si doivent estre retrouvez,
Par droit, sur Marion l'Idolle:
Une leçon de mon escolle
Leur liray, qui ne dure guere,
Teste n'ayent dure ne folle,
Escoutent, car c'est la derniere.

Beaulx enfans, vous perdez la plus
Belle rose de vo chappeau,
Mes clers pres prenans comme glus
Se vous allez a Montpipeau
Ou a Rueil gardez la peau,
Car pour s'esbatre en ces deux lieux
Cuidant que vaulsist le rappeau
Le perdit Colin de Cayeux.

Punishment is good for a person,
It shouldn't make you angry,
Two hundred and twenty lashes
I award him at the hands of Henry. *1643*

Item, I don't know what to give
The Hôtel-Dieu or poor hospitals,
Jokes would be untimely and out of place
For the poor have enough troubles, *1647*
Everybody throws them his crumb,
I gave the Mendicants my goose,
All they'll see of it is the bones,
To the little fellow the little sum. *1651*

Item, I give to my barber
Whose name is Colin Galerne,
Next door to herb-dealer Angelot,
A big block of ice (where from? the Marne): *1655*
In order to winter comfortably,
He's to press it to his guts,
If all winter he does this faithfully
Next summer he won't feel too hot. *1659*

Item, nothing to the Foundlings,
It's the lostlings I have to console,
Who always turn up again,
It seems, at Marion the Idol's: *1663*
A single lesson from my school
I'll read to them, it's very short,
Let them not be pigheaded or foolish,
But listen, it's the last they'll get. *1667*

Sweet children, you throw away
The prettiest rose in your caps,
Scholars with fingers stickier than glue,
If you travel to Montpipeau *1671*
Or Rueil watch out for your skin,
For acting up in these two places
Believing an appeal would work
Colin de Cayeux lost his. *1675*

Ce n'est pas ung jeu de trois mailles,
Ou va corps et peut estre l'ame,
Qui pert, riens n'y sont repentailles
Qu'on n'en meure a honte et diffame,
Et qui gaigne n'a pas a femme
Dido la royne de Cartage,
L'homme est donc bien fol et infame
Qui pour si peu couche tel gage.

Qu'ung chascun encore m'escoute,
On dit, et il est verité,
Que charterie se boit toute
Au feu l'yver, au bois l'esté:
S'argent avez il n'est enté
Mais le despendez tost et viste,
Qui en voyez vous herité?
Jamais mal acquest ne prouffite.

BALLADE

Car ou soies porteur de bulles,
Pipeur ou hasardeur de dez,
Tailleur de faulx coings et te brusles
Comme ceulx qui sont eschaudez,
Traistres parjurs de foy vuidez,
Soies larron, ravis ou pilles,
Ou en va l'acquest, que cuidez?
Tout aux tavernes et aux filles.

Ryme, raille, cymballe, luttes,
Comme fol fainctif eshontez,
Farce, broulle, joue des fleustes,
Fais es villes et es citez
Farces, jeux et moralitez,
Gaigne au berlanc, au glic, aux quilles,
Aussi bien va, or escoutez,
Tout aux tavernes et aux filles.

It isn't a three-penny game,
There where goes body and maybe soul,
For the loser, repentance can't help
If he dies in disgrace and shame, *1679*
And the winner doesn't get as bride
Dido the Queen of Carthage,
Therefore the man is worthless and wild
Who for so little risks so much. *1683*

Listen to me, everyone,
There's a saying, and it's true,
The wine-wagon man drinks all his load
Winter by the fire, summer in the woods: *1687*
If you have money you don't stash it down
But squander it all in a minute,
Who do you see inheriting it?
Ill-gotten gain turns to no good. *1691*

BALLADE

For whether you're a pardoner,
A hustler or shooter of dice,
Or counterfeiter burning yourself
Like the people who get heated up, *1695*
Perjured traitors who have no faith,
Whether a robber, pillager or thief,
Where does the booty go, do you think?
All to the taverns and the girls. *1699*

Rhyme, rail, jingle, pluck the lute,
Like a clownish, brazen mummer,
Act, play magic, blow the flute,
Put on in villages and cities *1703*
Farces, interludes, moralities,
Win at berlan, glic, and kayles,
It goes so soon, now listen to me,
All to the taverns and the girls. *1707*

De telz ordures te reculles,
Laboure, fauche champs et prez,
Sers et pense chevaux et mulles,
S'aucunement tu n'es lettrez
Assez auras, se prens en grez,
Mais se chanvre broyes ou tilles
Ne tens ton labour qu'as ouvrez,
Tout aux tavernes et aux filles?

Chausses, pourpoins esguilletez,
Robes, et toutes vos drappilles,
Ains que vous fassiez pis portez
Tout aux tavernes et aux filles.

A vous parle, compaings de galle,
Mal des ames et bien du corps,
Gardez vous tous de ce mau hasle
Qui noircist les gens quant sont mors,
Eschevez le, c'est ung mal mors,
Passez vous au mieulx que pourrez
Et pour Dieu soiez tous recors
Qu'une fois viendra que mourrez.

Item, je donne aux Quinze Vings,
Qu'autant vauldroit nommer Trois Cens,
De Paris non pas de Provins
Car a ceulx tenu je me sens,
Ilz auront et je m'y consens
Sans les estuys mes grans lunettes
Pour mettre a part aux Innocens
Les gens de bien des deshonnestes.

Icy n'y a ne ris ne jeu,
Que leur valut avoir chevances,
N'en grans liz de parement jeu,
Engloutir vins en grosses pances,
Mener joye, festes et dances
Et de ce prest estre a toute heure?
Toutes faillent telles plaisances
Et la coulpe si en demeure.

Keep well away from such trash,
Plow and mow the fields and meadows,
Groom and fodder horses and mules,
Even if you can't read or write, *1711*
You can live well, if you take it easy,
But if you hackle and scutch the hemp
Don't you just hand your working time over
All to the taverns and the girls? *1715*

Your britches and spangled doublets,
Your gowns and all your underwear,
Before you do worse turn them in
All to the taverns and the girls. *1719*

It's you I'm addressing, comrades in revels,
Sick in soul and well in body,
Beware all of you of this dry rot
That turns men black when they're dead, *1723*
Stay clear, it has a wicked bite,
As best you can try to get by
And for God's sake don't forget
A time will come when you will die. *1727*

Item, I give the Fifteen Score,
Whom you might as well call the Three Hundred,
The ones in Paris not Provins
Since it's them I'm indebted to, *1731*
They are to get, I here consent,
My eyeglasses without the case
For telling at the Innocents
The respectable people from the bad ones. *1735*

There's nothing to laugh at here,
Where did it get them, being rich,
Or to have lolled in big beds under canopies
Pouring down wine into potbellies, *1739*
Reveling, feasting and dancing,
Ready for more no matter when?
Pleasures like these all come to nothing
And the guilt of them remains. *1743*

Quant je considere ces testes
Entassees en ces charniers,
Tous furent maistres des requestes
Au moins de la Chambre aux Deniers
Ou tous furent portepanniers,
Autant puis l'ung que l'autre dire
Car d'evesques ou lanterniers
Je n'y congnois rien a redire.

Et icelles qui s'enclinoient
Unes contre autres en leurs vies
Desquelles les unes regnoient
Des autres craintes et servies,
La les voy toutes assouvies
Ensemble en ung tas peslemesle,
Seigneuries leur sont ravies,
Clerc ne maistre ne s'y appelle.

Or sont ilz mors, Dieu ait leurs ames,
Quant est des corps ilz sont pourris
Aient esté seigneurs ou dames
Souef et tendrement nourris
De cresme, fromentee ou riz
Et les os declinent on pouldre
Auxquelz ne chault d'esbatz ne ris,
Plaise au doulx Jhesus les absouldre.

Aux trespassez je fais ce laiz
Et icelluy je communique
A regens, cours, sieges, palaiz,
Hayneurs d'avarice l'inique,
Lesquelz pour la chose publique
Se seichent les os et les corps,
De Dieu et de saint Dominique
Soient absols quant seront mors.

Item, riens a Jacquet Cardon
Car je n'ay riens pour luy d'honneste,
(Non pas que le gette habandon)
Sinon ceste bergeronnette:

When I think about these skulls
Piled up in the boneyards,
Every one was Finance Minister
At least of the Royal Treasury *1747*
Or every one was a navvy,
I can say this or that just as well
Because, bishops or lantern-makers,
I don't see any way to tell. *1751*

And heads that used to snuggle
Up to others during their lives
Of whom a few used to hold sway
Over the rest who would cringe and serve, *1755*
I see them here appeased at last
Shoveled in a heap together,
Their powers have been ripped away,
Here no one's called clerk or master. *1759*

Now they're dead, God keep their souls,
As for their bodies these have rotted
Whether they used to be lords or ladies
Fully and lovingly fed *1763*
On whipped creams, puddings and rice
And the bones are falling to dust
No longer stirred by lust or laughter,
May the mild Jesus absolve them. *1767*

This is my legacy to the dead
And this same one I make over
To regents, courts, tribunes, palaces,
Enemies of the sin of greed, *1771*
Men who, serving the public good,
Dry out their bones and bodies,
By God and by Saint Dominic
May they be absolved when they die. *1775*

Item, nothing to Jacquet Cardon
For I've nothing decent to give him,
(Not that I'm cutting him off)
Other than this *bergeronnette:* *1779*

S'elle eust le chant "Marionnette"
Fait pour Marion la Peautarde
Ou d' "Ouvrez vostre huys, Guillemette"
Elle allast bien a la moustarde:

CHANSON

Au retour de dure prison
Ou j'ai laissié presque la vie,
Se Fortune a sur moy envie
Jugiez s'elle fait mesprison,
Il me semble que par raison
Elle deust bien estre assouvie
Au retour.

Ce cy plaine est de desraison
Qu'i vueille que du tout devie
Plaise a Dieu que l'ame ravie
En soit lassus en sa maison
Au retour.

Item, donne a maistre Lomer
Comme extraict que je suis de fee
Qu'il soit bien amé, mais d'amer
Fille en chief ou femme coeffee
Ja n'en ayt la teste eschauffee,
Et qu'il ne luy couste une noix
Faire ung soir cent fois la faffee
En despit d'Ogier le Danois.

Item, donne aux amans enfermes
Sans le laiz maistre Alain Chartier
A leurs chevez, de pleurs et lermes
Trestout fin plain, ung benoistier
Et ung petit brain d'esglantier
En tous temps vert pour guipillon
Pourveu qu'ilz diront ung psaultier
Pour l'ame du povre Villon.

If it went to the tune of "Marionette"
Composed for Marion la Peautarde
Or of "Open Your Door, Guillemette"
It would be tasty with mustard: *1783*

SONG

On my return from the harsh prison
In which I nearly lost my life,
If fortune still has it in for me *1786*
Judge if she is not mistaken,
It seems to me in all reason
She should be more than satisfied
On my return. *1790*

If she is so unreasonable
As to wish that I quit this life
May it please God my ravished soul
To gather into his mansion
On my return. *1795*

Item, I bequeath to Master Lomer
As I'm descended of the fairies
The gift of being loved, but let him not
Feel love for any woman *1799*
Who goes bareheaded or wears a hat
And let it not cost him a nut
To ball a hundred girls a night
And beat out Ogier the Dane. *1803*

Item, I give to the sick-with-love
Besides Alain Chartier's legacy
At their bedsides, with weeping and tears
Quickly filled, a holy-water basin *1807*
And a little sprig of eglantine
Forever green, as an aspergillum
Provided they recite a psalm
For the soul of the poor Villon. *1811*

Item, a maistre Jacques James
Qui se tue d'amasser biens
Donne fiancer tant de femmes
Qu'il vouldra, mais d'espouser riens:
Pour qui amasse il, pour les siens?
Il ne plaint fors que ses morceaulx,
Ce qui fut aux truyes je tiens
Qu'il doit de droit estre aux pourceaulx.

Item, le camus Seneschal
Qui une fois paya mes debtes,
En recompence, mareschal
Sera pour ferrer oes, canettes:
Je luy envoie ces sornettes
Pour soy desennuyer, combien
S'il veult, face en des alumettes,
De bien chanter s'ennuye on bien.

Item, au Chevalier du Guet
Je donne deux beaulx petiz pages,
Philebert et le gros Marquet,
Lesquelz servy, dont sont plus sages,
La plus partie de leurs aages,
Ont le prevost des mareschaulx
Helas, s'ilz sont cassez de gages
Aller les fauldra tous deschaulx.

Item, a Chappelain je laisse
Ma chappelle a simple tonsure
Chargiee d'une seiche messe
Ou il ne fault pas grant lecture:
Resigné luy eusse ma cure
Mais point ne veult de charge d'ames,
De confesser, ci dit, n'a cure
Sinon chamberieres et dames.

Pour ce que scet bien mon entente
Jehan de Calais, honnorable homme,
Qui ne me vit des ans a trente
Et ne scet comment je me nomme,

Item, to Master Jacques James
Who's killing himself to get rich
I give all the women he could want
As fiancées, but not one as wife: *1815*
Who does he get rich for, his kin?
He whines for nothing but his grub,
What was for the sow I reckon
Belongs by right to the pigs. *1819*

Item, the pug-nosed Seneschal
Who once paid off my debts for me,
Shall be made in recompense
The smith for shoeing geese and ducks: *1823*
I'm sending him these little jokes
To cheer him up, but if he likes
He can make them into matches,
Of good singing you can have too much. *1827*

Item, to the Captain of the Watch
I give two pretty little pages,
Philibert and fat Marquet,
Who serviced, and it made them wiser, *1831*
For the largest part of their lives,
The provost of the marshals,
Alas, if they've been laid off
They'll have to go all barefoot. *1835*

Item, I leave to Chappelain
My chapel of simple tonsure
Which entails saying a dry Mass
In which little reading is needed: *1839*
I'd have thrown in my curacy
But the care of souls isn't his line,
He has no taste, he says, for confessions
Except of chambermaids and ladies. *1843*

Because he knows my intent
Jean de Calais, a man of honor,
Who hasn't seen me in thirty years
And doesn't even know my name, *1847*

De tout ce testament, en somme,
S'aucun n'y a difficulté
L'oster jusqu'au rez d'une pomme
Je luy en donne faculté.

De le gloser et commenter,
De le diffinir et descripre,
Diminuer ou augmenter,
De le canceller et prescripre
De sa main et, ne sceut escripre,
Interpreter et donner sens
A son plaisir, meilleur ou pire,
A tout cecy je m'y consens.

Et s'aucun dont n'ay congnoissance
Estoit allé de mort a vie
Je vueil et luy donne puissance
Affin que l'ordre soit suyvie
Pour estre mieulx parassouvie
Que ceste aumosne ailleurs transporte
Sans se l'appliquer par envie,
A son ame je m'en rapporte.

Item, j'ordonne a Sainte Avoye
Et non ailleurs, ma sepulture
Et affin qu'un chascun me voie
Non pas en char mais en painture
Que l'on tire mon estature
D'ancre s'il ne coustoit trop chier,
De tombel? riens, je n'en ay cure
Car il greveroit le planchier.

Item, vueil qu'autour de ma fosse
Ce qui s'ensuit sans autre histoire
Soit escript en lettre assez grosse
Et qui n'auroit point d'escriptoire
De charbon ou de pierre noire
Sans en riens entamer le plastre
Au moins sera de moi memoire
Telle qu'elle est d'ung bon follastre:

To wit, anywhere in this will,
Should there be any difficulty
To pare it like an apple peel
I do give him authority. *1851*

To gloss it and to annotate it,
To define it and to fill it in,
To shorten it and to stretch it out,
To cross it off and to annul it, *1855*
With his own hand, and if he can't write,
To interpret it and to give it sense,
For better or worse, as he sees fit,
To all this I do here consent. *1859*

And if unbeknownst to me some heir
Has passed from death into life
I do will and empower Calais
So as to carry out the bequest *1863*
And see it properly fulfilled
To award the gift to someone else
Without keeping it in greed himself,
I leave it up to his conscience. *1867*

Item, I specify Sainte-Avoye
And nowhere else, for my sepulcher
And so that everyone may see me
Not in the flesh but in a painting *1871*
Let my full-length portrait be done
In ink if it isn't too dear,
A tombstone? I don't care for one
For it might overload the floor. *1875*

Item, I will that at my grave
The following words and only these
Be written in great big letters
And if there's no writing tool *1879*
Use charcoal or a lump of coal
Trying not to scratch the plaster,
At least a memory of me will remain
Such as it may be of a wild one: *1883*

EPITAPHE

Cy gist et dort en ce sollier
Qu'amours occist de son raillon
Ung povre petit escollier
Qui fut nommé Françoys Villon,
Oncques de terre n'eut sillon,
Il donna tout, chascun le scet,
Tables, tresteaulx, pain, corbeillon,
Pour Dieu, dictes en ce verset:

RONDEAU

Repos eternel donne a cil,
Sire, et clarté perpetuelle,
Qui vaillant plat ne escuelle
N'eut oncques, n'ung brain de percil,
Il fut rez, chief, barbe et sourcil
Comme ung navet qu'on ret ou pelle,
Repos eternel.

Rigueur le transmit en exil
Et luy frappa au cul la pelle
Non obstant qu'il dit, "J'en appelle!"
Qui n'est pas terme trop subtil,
Repos eternel.

Item, je vueil qu'on sonne a bransle
Le gros beffroy qui est de voirre
Combien qu'il n'est cuer qui ne tremble
Quant de sonner est a son erre:
Sauvé a mainte belle terre
Le temps passé, chascun le scet,
Fussent gens d'armes ou tonnerre
Au son de luy tout mal cessoit.

Les sonneurs auront quatre miches
Et se c'est peu, demye douzaine,
Autant n'en donnent les plus riches,
Mais ilz seront de saint Estienne:

EPITAPH

Here lies and sleeps in this garret
One slain by love's spur
A poor wretched scholar
Who was named François Villon, *1887*
He never owned a furrow on earth,
He gave it all away, everyone knows,
Tables, chairs, bread, basket,
Before God, say in these verses: *1891*

RONDEAU

Rest eternal grant him,
Lord, and everlasting light,
The price of a plate or a bowl *1894*
He never had, nor of a parsley sprig,
He was shaved, head, beard and eyebrows
Like some turnip you scrape or peel,
Rest eternal. *1898*

Harshness sent him into exile
And whacked him with a shovel on the ass
Even though he cried, "I appeal!"
Which isn't a very obscure phrase,
Rest eternal. *1903*

Item, I want them to toll full force
The big bell that's made of glass
Though there isn't a heart which doesn't quail
Whenever that ringing goes on: *1907*
Many fair lands it has saved
In times past, as everyone knows,
Whether armed men or thunder
At its sound all evil would cease. *1911*

The bellringers shall get four buns
And if this is too few, a half dozen,
Even the rich don't give you that many,
But they'll be the kind Saint Stephen got. *1915*

Vollant est homme de grant paine,
L'ung en sera (quant g'y regarde,
Il en vivra une sepmaine)
Et l'autre? Au fort, Jehan de la Garde.

Pour tout ce fournir et parfaire
J'ordonne mes executeurs
Auxquels fait bon avoir affaire
Et contentent bien leurs debteurs:
Ilz ne sont pas moult grans vanteurs
Et ont bien de quoy, Dieu mercis,
De ce fait seront directeurs,
Escry, je t'en nommerai six.

C'est maistre Martin Bellefaye,
Lieutenant du cas criminel,
Qui sera l'autre? G'y pensoye,
Ce sera sire Colombel,
S'il luy plaist et il luy est bel
Il entreprendra ceste charge,
Et l'autre? Michiel Jouvenel,
Ces trois, seulz et pour tout, j'en charge.

Mais ou cas qu'ilz s'en excusassent
En redoubtant les premiers frais
Ou totallement recusassent
Ceulx qui s'enssuivent cy après
Institue, gens de bien tres,
Phelip Brunel noble escuyer,
Et l'autre? son voisin d'emprès,
Si est maistre Jacques Raguier,

Et l'autre? maistre Jaques James,
Trois hommes de bien et d'onneur
Desirans de sauver leurs ames
Et doubtans Dieu Nostre Seigneur:
Plus tost y mecteront du leur
Que ceste ordonnance ne baillent,
Point n'auront de contrerolleur,
A leur bon seul plaisir en taillent.

Vollant is very assiduous,
He'll be one (as a matter of fact,
He'll live on it for a whole week)
The other? Jean de la Garde, of course. *1919*

To provide and carry out all this
I herewith name my executors
Whom it helps to get the business
And it also pleases their debtors: *1923*
They don't boast about being rich
And yet, thank God, they're in the chips
Which is why they'll be the directors,
Copy down, I will name you six. *1927*

One is Master Martin Bellefaye,
Lieutenant of cases criminal,
Who'll be second? I know already,
It will be Sire Colombel, *1931*
If he finds it amusing and agreeable
He'll take the responsibility,
And the third? Michel Jouvenel,
Once and for all I appoint these three. *1935*

But in the event they decline
Put off by the least expense
Or funk out completely
Those whose names appear below *1939*
I invest, men of true character,
Philippe Brunel the noble squire
And the second? his near neighbor,
It's Master Jacques Raguier, *1943*

And the third? Master Jacques James,
Three men of substance and honor
Who care for their souls' salvation
And stand in fear of God our Lord: *1947*
They'd sooner make good a loss themselves
Than default on this testament,
They won't be assigned any overseer
And can cut the cake as they want. *1951*

Des testamens qu'on dit le Maistre
De mon fait n'aura *quid* ne *quod,*
Mais ce sera ung jeune prestre
Qui est nommé Thomas Tricot:
Voulentiers beusse a son escot
Et qu'il me coustast ma cornete,
S'il sceust jouer a ung tripot
Il eust de moy *le Trou Perrete.*

Quant au regart du luminaire
Guillaume du Ru j'y commetz,
Pour porter les coings du suaire
Aux executeurs le remetz:
Trop plus mal me font qu'onques mais
Barbe, cheveulx, penil, sourcis,
Mal me presse, temps desormais
Que crie a toutes gens mercis.

BALLADE

A Chartreux et a Celestins,
A Mendians et a Devotes,
A musars et claquepatins,
A servans et filles mignotes
Portans surcotz et justes cotes,
A cuidereaux d'amours transsis
Chaussans sans meshaing fauves botes,
Je crie a toutes gens mercis.

A filletes monstrans tetins
Pour avoir plus largement hostes,
A ribleurs, mouveurs de hutins,
A bateleurs, traynans marmotes,
A folz, folles, a sotz et sotes
Qui s'en vont siflant six a six,
A marmosetz et mariotes,
Je crie a toutes gens mercis.

The so-called Master of Testaments
Won't get quid nor quod from this,
A young priest will handle it instead
By the name of Thomas Tricot: *1955*
I'd gladly have a drink on him
Except it might cost me my cornet,
If he knew how to make his strokes
He'd have had from me *Perrete's Hole.* *1959*

Concerning the funeral lights
I entrust this to Guillaume du Ru,
The matter of the pallbearers
I leave to the executors: *1963*
Worse than ever do they give me pain
Beard, hair, crotch and eyebrows,
My woes close in, time from now on
To cry to all men pardon. *1967*

BALLADE

To Carthusians and Celestines,
To Mendicants and Devotes,
To stargazers and clock-pattens,
To serving girls and pretty sluts *1971*
In jackets and tight-fitting coats,
To cocky beaux fainting with love
Happily fitted with tawny boots,
I cry to all men pardon. *1975*

To the girlies showing their bubs
To bring in a fatter clientele,
To toughs and starters of brawls,
To jugglers with monkey to heel, *1979*
To fools, follies, to clowns and clownettes
Who march whistling six in a line,
To puppets and to marionettes,
I cry to all men pardon. *1983*

Sinon aux traistres chiens matins
Qui m'ont fait chier dur et crostes
Maschier mains soirs et mains matins
Qu'ores je ne crains pas trois crotes:
Je feisse pour eulx petz et rotes,
Je ne puis car je suis assis,
Au fort, pour eviter riotes,
Je crie a toutes gens mercis.

Qu'on leur froisse les quinze costes
De gros mailletz fors et massis,
De plombees et telz pelotes,
Je crie a toutes gens mercis.

AUTRE BALLADE

Icy se clost le testament
Et finist du pauvre Villon,
Venez a son enterrement
Quant vous orrez le carillon
Vestus rouge com vermillon
Car en amours mourut, martir,
Ce jura il sur son couillon
Quant de ce monde voult partir.

Et je croy bien que pas n'en ment
Car chassié fut comme ung souillon
De ses amours hayneusement
Tant que d'icy a Roussillon
Brosse n'y a ne brossillon
Qui n'eust, ce dit il sans mentir,
Ung lambeau de son cotillon
Quant de ce monde voult partir.

Except to the sons-of-bitches
Who made me shit small and gnaw
Crusts many a dusk and dawn,
Who don't scare me now three turds: *1987*
I'd raise for them belches and farts
But I can't for I'm sitting down,
Instead, to prevent riots,
I cry to all men pardon. *1991*

May their fifteen ribs be mauled
With big hammers heavy and strong
And lead weights and similar balls,
I cry to all men pardon. *1995*

ANOTHER BALLADE

Here ends and finishes
The testament of poor Villon,
Come to his burial
When you hear the carillon *1999*
Dressed up in red-vermilion
For he died a martyr in love,
This he swore on his testicles
As he made his way out of this world. *2003*

And I think it isn't a lie
For he was chased like a scullion
By his loves so spitefully
That all the way to Roussillon *2007*
There isn't a bush or ravine
That didn't get, he tells the truth,
A strip of cloth from his back
As he made his way out of this world. *2011*

Il est ainsi, et tellement,
Quant mourut n'avoit qu'ung haillon,
Qui plus, en mourant, mallement
L'espoignoit d'amours l'esguillon,
Plus agu que le ranguillon
D'ung baudrier luy faisoit sentir,
C'est de quoy nous esmerveillon
Quant de ce monde voult partir.

Prince, gent comme esmerillon,
Sachiez qu'il fist au departir,
Ung traict but de vin morillon
Quant de ce monde voult partir.

This is how it was, so much so
He had only a rag when he died,
What's more, as he died, sorely
The spur of love was pricking him, *2015*
Sharper than the buckle-tongue
Of a baldric he could feel it,
And this is what we marvel at
As he made his way out of this world. *2019*

Prince, beautiful as a merlin,
Hear what he did as he left,
He took a long swig of dead-black wine
As he made his way out of this world. *2023*

POÉSIES DIVERSES

MISCELLANEOUS POEMS

POÉSIES DIVERSES

BALLADE

Hommes faillis, despourveuz de raison,
Desnaturez et hors de congnoissance,
Desmis du sens, comblez de desraison,
Fols abusez, plains de descongnoissance,
Qui procurez contre vostre naissance,
Vous soubzmettans a detestable mort
Par lascheté, las, que ne vous remort
L'orribleté qui a honte vous maine,
Voyez comment maint jeunes homs est mort
Par offenser et prendre autruy demaine.

Chascun en soy voye sa mesprison,
Ne nous venjons, prenons en pacience,
Nous congnoissons que ce monde est prison
Aux vertueux franchis d'impatience,
Battre, rouiller, pour ce n'est pas science,
Tollir, ravir, piller, meurtrir a tort,
De Dieu ne chault, trop de verté se tort
Qui en telz faiz sa jeunesse demaine
Dont a la fin ses poins doloreux tort
Par offenser et prendre autruy demaine.

Que vault piper, flater, rire en trayson,
Quester, mentir, affermer sans fiance,
Farcer, tromper, artifier poison,
Vivre en pechié, dormir en deffiance
De son prouchain sans avoir confiance?
Pour ce conclus, de bien faisons effort,
Reprenons cuer, ayons en Dieu confort,
Nous n'avons jour certain en la sepmaine,
De nos maulx ont noz parens le ressort
Par offenser et prendre autruy demaine.

MISCELLANEOUS POEMS

BALLADE

Twisted men dispossessed of reason,
Unnatural and fallen from knowledge,
Empty of sense and full of unreason,
Deluded fools stuffed with emptiness
Who hire out against your birthright *5*
Giving yourselves to detestable death
Through cowardice, alas, why no remorse
For the horror dragging you into shame,
See the way many young men die
Through wrongdoing and taking from others. *10*

Let everybody see his guilt within,
Let us not seek revenge, let us have patience,
We recognize this world is a prison
For virtuous men freed of impatience,
To fight or brawl, therefore, makes no sense, *15*
To steal, rape, pillage, or kill wrongfully,
He cares not for God and turns his back on virtue
Who spends his youth in such adventures
For which at last he wrings his hands in sorrow
Through wrongdoing and taking from others. *20*

Why connive, flatter, snigger behind backs,
Hawk indulgences, lie, pledge in bad faith,
Hustle, cheat, concoct poison,
Live deep in sin, sleep in suspicion
Of your neighbor and not have any trust? *25*
So I end: let us strive for the good,
Let us take heart and find our strength in God,
Not a day in the week can we feel secure,
Our families take the brunt of our blows
Through wrongdoing and taking from others. *30*

Vivons en paix, exterminons discort,
Ieunes et vieulx, soyons tous d'ung accort,
La loy le veult, l'apostre le ramaine
Licitement en l'epistre rommaine,
Ordre nous fault, estat ou aucun port,
Notons ces poins, ne laissons le vray port
Par offenser et prendre autruy demaine.

BALLADE

Tant grate chievre que mal gist,
Tant va le pot a l'eaue qu'il brise,
Tant chauffe on le fer qu'il rougist,
Tant le maille on qu'il se debrise,
Tant vault l'homme comme on le prise,
Tant s'eslongne il qu'il n'en souvient,
Tant mauvais est qu'on le desprise,
Tant crie l'on Noel qu'il vient.

Tant parle on qu'on se contredist,
Tant vault bon bruyt que grace acquise,
Tant promet on qu'on s'en desdist,
Tant prie on que chose est acquise,
Tant plus est chiere et plus est quise,
Tant la quiert on qu'on y parvient,
Tant plus commune et moins requise,
Tant crie l'on Noel qu'il vient.

Tant ayme on chien qu'on le nourrist,
Tant court chanson qu'elle est apprise,
Tant garde on fruit qu'il se pourrist,
Tant bat on place qu'elle est prise,
Tant tarde on que faut entreprise,
Tant se haste on que mal advient,
Tant embrasse on que chiet la prise,
Tant crie l'on Noel qu'il vient.

Let us live in peace, do away with discord,
Young and old, let us be in agreement,
The law commands it, the apostle states it
Explicitly in his Epistle to the Romans,
We must have order, degree, something to lean on, *35*
Let us take heed, let us not leave the true haven
Through wrongdoing and taking from others.

BALLADE

So much the goat scratches he can't sleep,
So much the pot takes water it breaks,
So much you heat iron it turns red,
So much you hammer it it cracks, *4*
So much a man's worth as he's esteemed,
So much is he away he's forgotten,
So much is he bad he's despised,
So much you cry Noël that it comes. *8*

So much you talk you contradict yourself,
So much fame's worth as it gets you favors,
So much you promise you take it back,
So much you beg you're given what you sought, *12*
So much a thing's expensive everyone wants it,
So much you go after it you get it,
So much it's common it loses its charm,
So much you cry Noël that it comes. *16*

So much you love a dog you feed it,
So much a song's heard it catches on,
So much fruit's hoarded up it goes rotten,
So much you dispute a place it's already taken, *20*
So much you dawdle you ruin your life,
So much you hurry you run out of luck,
So much you hold on you lose your grip,
So much you cry Noël that it comes. *24*

Tant raille on que plus on n'en rit,
Tant despent on qu'on n'a chemise,
Tant est on franc que tout y frit,
Tant vault "tien" que chose promise,
Tant ayme on Dieu qu'on suit l'Eglise,
Tant donne on qu'emprunter convient,
Tant tourne vent qu'il chiet en bise,
Tant crie l'on Noel qu'il vient.

Prince, tant vit fol qu'il s'avise,
Tant va il qu'après il revient,
Tant le mate on qu'il se ravise,
Tant crie l'on Noel qu'il vient.

BALLADE

Je congnois bien mouches en let,
Je congnois a la robe l'homme,
Je congnois le beau temps du let,
Je congnois au pommier la pomme,
Je congnois l'arbre a veoir la gomme,
Je congnois quant tout est de mesmes,
Je congnois qui besongne ou chomme,
Je congnois tout fors que moy mesmes.

Je congnois pourpoint au colet,
Je congnois le moyne a la gonne,
Je congnois le maistre au varlet.
Je congnois au voille la nonne,
Je congnois quant pipeur jargonne,
Je congnois fols nourris de cresmes,
Je congnois le vin a la tonne,
Je congnois tout fors que moy mesmes.

Je congnois cheval et mulet,
Je congnois leur charge et leur somme,
Je congnois Bietris et Belet,
Je congnois get qui nombre et somme,

So much you joke you quit laughing,
So much you spend you lose your shirt,
So much you're honest you go broke,
So much is "here" worth as a thing promised, *28*
So much you love God you go to church,
So much you give you're obliged to borrow,
So much the wind shifts it blows cold at last,
So much you cry Noël that it comes. *32*

Prince, so much a fool lives he wises up,
So much he travels he comes back home,
So much they beat him he knows he was wrong,
So much you cry Noël that it comes. *36*

BALLADE

I know flies in milk,
I know the man by what he wears,
I know fair weather from foul,
I know the apple by the tree, *4*
I know the tree by the look of the sap,
I know when all things are the same,
I know who labors and who loafs,
I know all things except myself. *8*

I know the doublet by the collar,
I know the monk by the cowl,
I know the master by the servant,
I know the nun by the veil, *12*
I know when hustlers start their spiel,
I know delinquents raised on cream,
I know the wine by the barrel,
I know all things except myself. *16*

I know the horse and the mule,
I know their limit and their load,
I know Beatrice and Belle,
I know beads that count and add, *20*

Je congnois vision et somme,
Je congnois la faulte des Boesmes,
Je congnois le povoir de Romme,
Je congnois tout fors que moy mesmes.

Prince, je congnois tout en somme,
Je congnois coulourez et blesmes,
Je congnois Mort quit tout consomme,
Je congnois tout fors que moy mesmes.

BALLADE

Il n'est soing que quant on a fain
Ne service que d'ennemy
Ne maschier qu'ung botel de foing
Ne fort guet que d'homme ondormy
Ne clemence que felonnie
N'asseurence que de peureux
Ne foy que d'homme qui regnie
Ne bien conseillé qu'amoureux.

Il n'est engendrement qu'en boing
Ne bon bruit que d'homme banny
Ne ris qu'après ung coup de poing
Ne lotz que debtes mettre en ny
Ne vraye amour qu'en flaterie
N'encontre que de maleureux
Ne vray rapport que menterie
Ne bien conseillé qu'amoureux.

Ne tel repos que vivre en soing
N'honneur porter que dire, "Fi!"
Ne soy vanter que de faulx coing
Ne santé que d'homme bouffy
Ne hault vouloir que couardie
Ne conseil que de furieux
Ne doulceur qu'en femme estourdie
Ne bien conseillé qu'amoureux.

I know sleep and I know dreams,
I know the Bohemians' heresy,
I know the power of Rome,
I know all things except myself. *24*

Prince, I know everything in brief,
I know the red-cheeked and the pale,
I know Death who devours all,
I know all things except myself. *28*

BALLADE

There's no care but when you're hungry
Nor good deed but from the enemy
Nor any food but baled hay
Nor sharp lookout but a man asleep *4*
Nor mercy but a felony
Nor security but from the frightened
Nor good faith but from an atheist
Nor any wise counsel but from lovers. *8*

There's no conceiving but in baths
Nor good reputations but for the exiled
Nor laughs but from getting slapped
Nor praise but from not paying debts *12*
Nor true love but in flattery
Nor encounters but of the miserable
Nor real understanding but through lies
Nor any wise counsel but from lovers. *16*

There's no way to rest but to worry
Nor to bestow honor but to say "Baloney!"
Nor generosity but with counterfeit money
Nor good health but elephantiasis *20*
Nor noble resolve but to shirk
Nor good advice but from maniacs
Nor gentleness but from wild women
Nor any wise counsel but from lovers. *24*

Voulez vous que verté vous die?
Il n'est jouer qu'en maladie,
Lettre vraye que tragedie,
Lasche homme que chevalereux,
Orrible son que melodie
Ne bien conseillé qu'amoureux.

BALLADE

Rencontré soit des bestes feu getans
Que Jason vit querant la toison d'or
Ou transmué d'homme en beste sept ans
Ainsi que fut Nabugodonosor
Ou perte il ait et guerre aussi villaine
Que les Troyens pour la prinse d'Helaine
Ou avallé soit avec Tantalus
Et Proserpine aux infernaulx palus
Ou plus que Job soit en griefve souffrance
Tenant prison en la tour Dedalus
Qui mal vouldroit au royaulme de France.

Quatre mois soit en ung vivier chantans
La teste au fons ainsi que le butor
Ou au Grant Turc vendu deniers contans
Pour estre mis au harnois comme ung tor
Ou trente ans soit comme la Magdalaine
Sans drap vestir de linge ne de laine
Ou soit noyé comme fut Narcisus
Ou aux cheveulx comme Absalon pendus
Ou comme fut Judas par Desperance
Ou puist perir comme Simon Magus
Qui mal vouldroit au royaulme de France.

D'Octovien puist revenir le tems
C'est qu'on luy coule au ventre son tresor
Ou qu'il soit mis entre meules flotans
En ung moulin comme fut saint Victor
Ou transglouty en la mer sans aleine

Shall I tell you the truth?
There's no delight but in sickness
Nor true story but a tragedy
Nor coward but a knight-at-arms *28*
Nor hideous noise but music
Nor any wise counsel but from lovers.

BALLADE

May he run into the beasts that belch fire
Which Jason saw, seeking the Golden Fleece,
Or be changed from man to beast for seven years
As Nebuchadnezzar was
Or may he know loss and war as cruel
As did the Trojans for the rape of Helen *6*
Or be swallowed along with Tantalus
And Proserpine into the swamps of Hell
Or may he be afflicted worse than Job
Locked up in Daedalus' Tower
He who wishes ill against the kingdom of France. *11*

May he sing four months in a fishpond
Head touching bottom like the bittern
Or be sold for cash to the Grand Turk
And be strapped into harness like a bull
Or like Magdalene go for thirty years
Without any clothing of linen or wool *17*
Or may he drown the way Narcissus did
Or like Absalom be hanged by his hair
Or like Judas hang by Despair
Or may he perish as did Simon Magus
He who wishes ill against the kingdom of France. *22*

Let Octavian's time be brought back
That they may pour the Treasury into his belly
Or let him be lashed between turning stones
In a mill the way Saint Victor was
Or be engulfed by the sea unable to breathe

Pis que Jonas ou corps de la baleine
Ou soit banny de la clarté Phebus,
Des biens Juno et du soulas Venus
Et du dieu Mars soit pugny a oultrance
Ainsy que fut roy Sardanapalus
Qui mal vouldroit au royaulme de France.

Prince, porté soit des serfs Eolus
En la forest ou domine Glaucus
Ou privé soit de paix et d'esperance
Car digne n'est de posseder vertus
Qui mal vouldroit au royaulme de France.

BALLADE

Je meurs de seuf auprès de la fontaine,
Chault comme feu et tremble dent a dent,
En mon païs suis en terre loingtaine,
Lez ung brasier frissonne tout ardent,
Nu comme ung ver, vestu en president,
Je ris en pleurs et attens sans espoir,
Confort reprens en triste desespoir,
Je m'esjouïs et n'ay plaisir aucun,
Puissant je suis sans force et sans povoir,
Bien recueully, debouté de chascun.

Rien ne m'est seur que la chose incertaine,
Obscur, fors ce qui est tout evident,
Doubte ne fais fors en chose certaine,
Science tiens a soudain accident,
Je gaigne tout et demeure perdent,
Au point du jour dis, "Dieu vous doint bon soir",
Gisant envers j'ay grant paour de cheoir,
J'ay bien de quoy et si n'en ay pas ung,
Eschoitte attens et d'omme ne suis hoir,
Bien recueully, debouté de chascun.

Worse off than Jonah inside the whale *28*
Or may he be banished from Phoebus' light,
From Juno's bounties and from the solaces of Venus
And be put through the punishments of Mars
As King Sardanapalus was
He who wishes ill against the kingdom of France. *33*

Prince, may Aeolus' lackeys take him up
And drop him in the "forest" where Glaucus reigns
Or may he be deprived of peace and hope
For he isn't fit to have virtues,
He who wishes ill against the kingdom of France. *38*

BALLADE

I die of thirst beside the fountain,
Hot as fire I'm shaking tooth on tooth,
In my own country I'm in a distant land,
Beside the blaze I'm shivering in flames,
Naked as a worm, dressed like a president, *5*
I laugh in tears and hope despairingly,
I cheer up in a sad despair,
I'm joyful and nothing gives me pleasure,
I'm strong and haven't any force or power,
Warmly welcomed, rebuffed by everyone. *10*

I'm sure of nothing but the uncertain,
Baffled by nothing but the evident,
I'm doubtful of nothing but the sure,
I regard knowledge as mere accident,
I always win and I remain the loser, *15*
At dawn I say, "I wish you good night,"
When lying down I'm afraid of falling,
I'm very rich and haven't a cent,
I await an inheritance and am no one's heir,
Warmly welcomed, rebuffed by everyone. *20*

De riens n'ay soing si mectz toute ma paine
D'acquerir biens et n'y suis pretendent,
Qui mieulx me dit c'est cil qui plus m'attaine
Et qui plus vray lors plus me va bourdent,
Mon amy est qui me fait entendent
D'ung signe blanc que c'est ung corbeau noir
Et qui me nuyst croy qu'il m'ayde a povoir,
Bourde, verté, au jour d'uy m'est tout un,
Je retiens tout, rien ne sçay concepvoir,
Bien recueully, debouté de chascun.

Prince clement, or vous plaise sçavoir
Que j'entens moult et n'ay sens ne sçavoir,
Parcial suis a toutes loys commun,
Que fais je plus? Quoy? Les gaiges ravoir!
Bien recueully, debouté de chascun.

ÉPITRE A MARIE D'ORLÉANS

Jam nova progenies celo demittitur alto.

O louee conception
Envoiee ça jus des cieulx,
Du noble lis digne syon,
Don de Jhesus tres precieulx,
Marie, nom tres gracieulx,
Fons de pitié, source de grace,
La joye, confort de mes yeulx,
Qui nostre paix bastist et brasse.

La paix, c'est assavoir, des riches,
Des povres le substantement,
Le rebours des felons et chiches,
Tres necessaire enfantement,
Conceu, porté honnestement
Hors le pechié originel,
Que dire je puis sainctement
Souvrain bien de Dieu eternel.

I never work and yet I go all out
To acquire wealth which I don't want,
Who speaks most kindly irritates me most,
Most truthfully will lie to me the most,
The person is my friend who makes me think *25*
That a white swan is a black crow,
He who harms me thinks he helps me out,
Falsehood, truth, to me they're both the same,
I remember all things and can't conceive of one,
Warmly welcomed, rebuffed by everyone. *30*

Merciful Prince, may it please you to know
I understand much and have no sense or learning,
A rare bird, I'm common before the law,
What's left to do? Set eyes on my pawned goods again!
Warmly welcomed, rebuffed by everyone. *35*

EPISTLE TO MARIE D'ORLÉANS

Jam nova progenies celo demittitur alto.

O blessed conception
Sent down to us out of heaven,
The noble lily's worthy scion,
Most precious gift of Jesus, *4*
Marie, in name so gracious,
Fountain of pity, spring of grace,
The joy and comfort of my eyes,
Who brings about and keeps our peace. *8*

Peace, that is, for the rich,
Sustenance for the poor,
Deadend for the false and mean,
Most necessary childbirth, *12*
Conceived and borne immaculately
Without original sin,
Whom in all piety I can call
The chief good of God eternal. *16*

Nom recouvré, joye de peuple,
Confort des bons, de maulx retraicte,
Du doulx seigneur premiere et seule
Fille de son cler sang extraicte,
Du dextre costé Clovis traicte,
Glorieuse ymage en tous fais
Ou hault ciel creee et pourtraicte
Pour esjouÿr et donner paix.

En l'amour et crainte de Dieu
Es nobles flans Cesar conceue,
Des petis et grans en tout lieu
A tres grande joye receue,
De l'amour Dieu traicte, tissue,
Pour les discordez ralier
Et aux enclos donner yssue,
Leurs lians et fers deslier.

Aucunes gens qui bien peu sentent,
Nourris en simplesse et confis,
Contre le vouloir Dieu attentent,
Par ignorance desconfis,
Desirans que feussiez ung fils,
Mais qu'ainsi soit, ainsi m'aist Dieux,
Je croy que ce soit grans proufis,
Raison, Dieu fait tout pour le mieulx.

Du Psalmiste je prens les dis,
Delectasti me, Domine,
In factura tua, si dis,
Noble enfant, de bonne heure né,
A toute doulceur destiné,
Manne du Ciel, celeste don,
De tout bienfait le guerdonné
Et de noz maulx le vray pardon.

Name found again, the people's joy,
Comfort of the good, haven from harm,
Of the dear lord the first and only
Daughter born of his illustrious blood, *20*
Sprung from Clovis' right side,
Image glorious in every way
Created and devised in heaven
To cause rejoicing and bring peace. *24*

In reverence and fear of God
Conceived in Caesar's noble flanks,
By small and great men everywhere
Received with wild rejoicing, *28*
Designed and woven of God's love
To unite all warring factions
And liberate all prisoners
Releasing their fetters and chains. *32*

Some who understand little,
Brought up simple and credulous,
Entertain hopes against God's will,
Ignorance having debased them, *36*
By wishing it had been a son,
But so help me God, the way it turned out
I believe was all to the good,
Because God does all for the best. *40*

From the Psalmist I take the phrase,
Delectasti me, Domine,
In factura tua, so I say,
Noble child born at an auspicious hour, *44*
Destined for all gentleness,
Celestial gift, manna from heaven,
Recompense of all good deeds
And the true pardon of our wrongs. *48*

DOUBLE BALLADE

Combien que j'ay leu en ung dit,
Inimicum putes, y a,
Qui te presentem laudabit,
Toutesfois, non obstant cela,
Oncques vray homme ne cela
En son courage aucun grant bien
Qui ne le montrast ça et la,
On doit dire du bien le bien.

Saint Jehan Baptiste ainsy le fist
Quant l'Aignel de Dieu descela,
En ce faisant pas ne mesfist
Dont sa voix es tourbes vola
De quoy saint Andry Dieu loua
Qui de lui cy ne sçavoit rien
Et au Fils de Dieu s'aloua,
On doit dire du bien le bien.

Envoiee de Jhesuschrist
Rappeller ça jus par deça
Les povres que Rigueur proscript
Et que Fortune betourna,
Si sçay bien comment il m'en va,
De Dieu, de vous, vie je tien,
Benoist celle qui vous porta,
On doit dire du bien le bien.

Cy, devant Dieu, fais congnoissance
Que creature feusse morte
Ne feust vostre doulce naissance
En charité puissant et forte
Qui ressuscite et reconforte
Ce que Mort avoit prins pour sien,
Vostre presence me conforte,
On doit dire du bien le bien.

DOUBLE BALLADE

Although I've read in a text,
Inimicum putes, it states,
Qui te presentem laudabit,
Nevertheless, in spite of this, *52*
No true man has ever hidden
Knowledge of great good in his breast
Who didn't show it here and there,
Of the good the good should be spoken. *56*

Saint John the Baptist did this
When he revealed the Lamb of God
And he was right in doing so
For his voice swayed the multitude *60*
Making Saint André praise God
Having been ignorant of Him
And devote himself to His Son,
Of the good the good should be spoken. *64*

Envoy sent by Jesus Christ
As a reminder in the world below
To wretches proscribed by Rigor
And buffeted by Fortune, *68*
Thus I know how it is with me,
I hold my life of God and you,
Blessed be she who gave you birth,
Of the good the good should be spoken. *72*

Here before God I acknowledge
I'd be a dead creature by now
Were it not for your sweet birth
Powerful and strong in charity *76*
Which revives and encourages
What Death had marked for his own,
Your presence here gives me strength,
Of the good the good should be spoken. *80*

Cy vous rans toute obeÿssance,
A ce faire Raison m'exorte,
De toute ma povre puissance,
Plus n'est deul qui me desconforte
N'aultre ennuy de quelconque sorte,
Vostre je suis et non plus mien,
A ce Droit et Devoir m'enhorte,
On doit dire du bien le bien.

O grace et pitié tres immense,
L'entree de paix et la porte,
Some de benigne clemence
Qui noz faultes toult et supporte,
Se de vous louer me deporte
Ingrat suis et je le maintien
Dont en ce refrain me transporte,
On doit dire du bien le bien.

Princesse, ce loz je vous porte
Que sans vous je ne feusse rien,
A vous et a tous m'en rapporte,
On doit dire du bien le bien.

Euvre de Dieu, digne, louee
Autant que nulle creature,
De tous biens et vertus douee
Tant d'esperit que de nature
Que de ceulx qu'on dit d'adventure
Plus que rubis noble ou balais,
Selon de Caton l'escripture,
Patrem insequitur proles.

Port asseuré, maintien rassiz
Plus que ne peut nature humaine,
Et eussiez des ans trente six
Enfance en rien ne vous demaine,
Que jour ne le die et sepmaine
Je ne sçay qui le me deffant,
A ce propos ung dit ramaine,
"De saige mere saige enfant."

I pledge you all obedience,
Reason urges me to do so,
To the best of my poor power,
No further woes can oppress me *84*
Or troubles of whatever sort,
I am yours, no longer my own,
This is what Right and Duty exhort,
Of the good the good should be spoken. *88*

O immense grace and pity,
Gateway and portal to peace,
Summit of sweet clemency
Which annuls and accepts our flaws: *92*
If I held back from giving praise
I'd be an ingrate I believe
And so I turn again to the phrase,
Of the good the good should be spoken. *96*

Princess, I offer you this eulogy,
Without you I would be nothing,
To you and everyone I say again,
Of the good the good should be spoken. *100*

God's handiwork, worthy, blessed
More than any earthly creature,
Gifted with all goods and virtues
As much in spirit and in nature *104*
As those who are sometimes called
Nobler and redder than rubies,
Or as it has been put by Cato,
Patrem insequitur proles. *108*

Safe harbor, stronghold calmer
Than human nature may achieve,
You could easily be thirty-six
You show so little childishness,
From saying this all day and all week
I don't know who's stopping me,
I offer a proverb on the subject,
"From a wise mother a wise child." *116*

Dont resume ce que j'ay dit,
Nova progenies celo,
Car c'est du poëte le dit,
Jamjam demittitur alto,
Saige Cassandre, belle Echo,
Digne Judith, caste Lucresse,
Je vous cognois, noble Dido,
A ma seule dame et maistresse.

En priant Dieu, digne pucelle,
Qu'il vous doint longue et bonne vie,
Qui vous ayme, ma damoiselle,
Ja ne coure sur luy envie,
Entiere dame et assouvie,
J'espoir de vous servir ainçoys,
Certes, se Dieu plaist, que devie
Vostre povre escolier Françoys.

EPISTRE

Aiez pitié, aiez pitié de moy,
A tout le moins, si vous plaist, mes amis,
En fosse gis non pas soubz houx ne may
En cest exil ouquel je suis transmis
Par Fortune comme Dieu l'a permis:
Filles, amans, jeunes gens et nouveaulx,
Danceurs, saulteurs faisans les piez de veaux
Vifz comme dars, agus comme aguillon,
Gousiers tintans cler comme cascaveaux,
Le lesserez la, le povre Villon?

Chantres chantans a plaisance sans loy,
Galans rians, plaisans en fais et dis,
Courens alans, francs de faulx or, d'aloy,
Gens d'esperit, ung petit estourdis,
Trop demourez car il meurt entandis:

So I sum up what I've said,
Nova progenies celo,
These are the poet's very words,
Jamjam demittitur alto, 120
Wise Cassandra, beautiful Echo,
Worthy Judith, chaste Lucrece,
I know you, noble Dido,
As my only lady and mistress. 124

And I pray God, worthy virgin,
That He give you long and happy life
And that whoever loves you, my lady,
Never be overcome by greed: 128
Perfect and fulfilled lady,
I hope to serve you before the time,
If God pleases, death shall take
Your poor scholar François. 132

EPISTLE

Have pity, have pity on me,
You, at least, who are my friends,
I lie in a dungeon not under holly or hawthorn
In this exile into which I was sent
By Fortune and by the leave of God: 5
Girls, lovers, young and fresh folk,
Hoofers and tumblers who dance the calf-step
Swift as arrows and sharp as spurs,
Throats tinkling clear as chimes,
Will you leave him here, the poor Villon? 10

Singers singing what strikes your fancy,
Happy gallants, pleasing in word and deed,
Gay dogs, free of false gold or alloy,
Witty fellows, a bit scatterbrained,
You wait too long for meanwhile he is dying: 15

Faiseurs de laiz, de motetz et rondeaux,
Quant mort sera vous lui ferez chaudeaux,
Ou gist, il n'entre escler ne tourbillon,
De murs espoix on lui a fait bandeaux,
Le lesserez la, le povre Villon?

Venez le veoir en ce piteux arroy,
Nobles hommes, francs de quart et de dix
Qui ne tenez d'empereur ne de roy
Mais seulement de Dieu de Paradis,
Jeuner lui fault dimenches et merdis
Dont les dens a plus longues que ratteaux,
Après pain sec non pas après gasteaux
En ses boyaulx verse eaue a gros bouillon,
Bas en terre table n'a ne tresteaulx,
Le lesserez la, le povre Villon?

Princes nommez, ancïens, jouvenceaux,
Impetrez moy graces et royaulx seaux
Et me montez en quelque corbillon,
Ainsi le font, l'un a l'autre, pourceaux
Car ou l'un brait ilz fuyent a monceaux,
Le lesserez la, le povre Villon?

REQUESTE A MONS. DE BOURBON

Le mien seigneur et prince redoubté,
Fleuron de lys, royalle geniture,
Françoys Villon que Travail a dompté
A coups orbes, par force de bature,
Vous supplie par ceste humble escripture
Que lui faciez quelque gracieux prest,
De s'obliger en toutes cours est prest
Si ne doubtez que bien ne vous contente
Sans y avoir dommaige n'interest,
Vous n'y perdez seulement que l'attente.

Composers of lays, of *motets* and *rondeaux*,
After he's dead you'll show up with his gruel,
Lightning and whirlwinds don't reach where he's lying,
He's been blindfolded with thick stone walls,
Will you leave him here, the poor Villon? *20*

Come to see him in this wretched state,
Noblemen, exempt from tax and tithe
Who do not hold of emperors or kings
But only of the God of Paradise,
On Sundays and Tuesdays he has to fast *25*
So that his teeth are longer than a rake's,
After dry bread never after cakes
He pours floods of water into his bowels,
Deep underground he hasn't table or bed,
Will you leave him here, the poor Villon? *30*

Princes named above, old men and young,
Obtain for me pardons and royal seals
And hoist me out of here in a basket,
This much the pigs do for each other
For if one squeals the rest come running in droves, *35*
Will you leave him here, the poor Villon?

REQUEST TO MONSIEUR DE BOURBON

My lord and redoubtable prince,
Fleur-de-lys of royal lineage,
François Villon whom suffering has quelled
With dull blows, by force of beatings,
Begs you in this humble letter
To let him have a gracious loan,
He'll engage for the debt in any court
So fear not, you'll be repaid
Without any loss or interest,
All you will lose will be the waiting. *10*

A prince n'a ung denier emprunté
Fors a vous seul, vostre humble creature,
De six escus que luy avez presté
Cela pieça il meist en nourriture,
Tout se paiera ensemble, c'est droiture,
Mais ce sera legierement et prest
Car se du glan rencontre en la forest
D'entour Patay et chastaignes ont vente
Paié serez sans delay ny arrest,
Vous n'y perdrez seulement que l'attente.

Se je peusse vendre de ma santé
A ung Lombart, usurier par nature,
Faulte d'argent m'a si fort enchanté
Que j'en prendroie ce cuide l'adventure,
Argent ne pens a gippon n'a sainture,
Beau sire Dieux, je m'esbaïs que c'est
Que devant moy croix ne se comparoist
Si non de bois ou pierre, que ne mente,
Mais s'une fois la vraye m'apparoist
Vous n'y perdrez seulement que l'attente.

Prince du lys qui a tout bien complaist
Que cuidez vous comment il me desplaist
Quant je ne puis venir a mon entente?
Bien m'entendez, aidez moy, s'il vous plaist,
Vous n'y perdrez seulement que l'attente.

Au dos de la lettre.

Allez, lettres, faictes ung sault,
Combien que n'ayez pié ne langue
Remonstrez en vostre harangue
Que faulte d'argent si m'assault.

He's never borrowed from any prince
But you, and is your humble servant,
As for the six *écus* you lent him once
A while back he put them into food,
He'll pay both debts at once, this is just, 15
And he'll do it with speed and dispatch
For if he finds acorns in the forest
Near Patay and can sell them for chestnuts
You'll get paid without stalling or delay,
All you will lose will be the waiting. 20

If I could sell a little of my health
To some born usurer of a Lombard
I'm so desperate for money
I think I'd even run this risk,
Money's not hanging from my belt or vest, 25
Good Lord God, what amazes me is
The only times I ever see a cross
It's made out of stone or wood, I swear,
If only the true one would appear
All you will lose will be the waiting. 30

Prince of the Lily complete in every good
What do you think of my anger
At failing to get the thing I want?
You understand me, help me, if you please,
All you will lose will be the waiting. 35

On the back of the letter

Go my letter, make a dash,
Although you haven't feet or tongue
Make it known in your harangue
That I'm beset by lack of cash. 39

LE DEBAT DU CUER ET DU CORPS DE VILLON

Qu'est ce que j'oy? – *Ce suis je.* – Qui? – *Ton cuer,*
Qui ne tient mais qu'a ung petit filet,
Force n'ay plus, substance ne liqueur,
Quant je te voy retraict ainsi seulet
Com povre chien tapy en reculet.
Pour quoy est ce, pour ta folle plaisance? –
Que t'en chault il? – *J'en ay la desplaisance.* –
Laisse m'en paix. – *Pour quoy?* – J'y penserai. –
Quant sera ce? – Quant seray hors d'enfance. –
Plus ne t'en dis. – Et je m'en passeray. –

Que penses tu? – Estre homme de valeur. –
Tu as trente ans, c'est l'aage d'un mullet,
Est ce enfance? – Nennil. – *C'est donc folleur*
Qui te saisist? – Par ou? Par le collet? –
Rien ne congnois. – Si fais. – *Quoy?* – Mouche en let,

L'ung est blanc, l'autre est noir, c'est la distance. –
Est ce donc tout? – Que veulx tu que je tance?
Se n'est assez, je recommenceray. –
Tu es perdu. – J'y mettray resistance. –
Plus ne t'en dis. – Et je m'en passeray. –

J'en ay le dueil, toy le mal et douleur,
Se feusses ung povre ydiot et folet
Encore eusses de t'excuser couleur,
Si n'as tu soing, tout t'est ung, bel ou let,
Ou la teste as plus dure qu'ung jalet
Ou mieulx te plaist qu'onneur ceste meschance.
Que respondras a ceste consequence? –
J'en seray hors quant je trespasseray. –
Dieu, quel confort. – Quelle sage eloquence. –
Plus ne t'en dis. – Et je m'en passeray. –

THE DEBATE BETWEEN VILLON'S HEART AND BODY

Who's that I hear? *It's me.* Who? *Your heart,*
That hangs on only by a tiny thread.
It takes away my strength, substance and sap,
To see you withdrawn this way all alone
Like a whipped cur sulking in a corner. 5
Why is it, because of your lust for pleasure?
What's it to you? *I get the displeasure.*
Let me alone. *Why?* I'll give you an answer.
When will you do that? When I've grown up.
I've nothing more to say. I'll manage without it. 10

What do you have in mind? To get somewhere.
You're thirty, a lifetime for a mule,
And you call that childhood? No. *Then madness*
Has hold of you. By what, the collar?
You don't know anything. Yes I do. *What?* Flies
in milk, 15
One's white, one's black, that's the difference.
And that's it? What do you want, an argument?
If that's not enough I'll begin again.
You're lost. I'll go down fighting.
I've nothing more to say. I'll manage without it. 20

I get the heartache, you the harm and pain.
If you were just some poor mixed-up nitwit
I'd be able to make excuses for you,
But you don't care, it's all one to you, foul or fair,
Either your head's harder than a rock 25
Or else you actually prefer misery to honor,
How do you answer this argument?
As soon as I'm dead it won't bother me.
God, what comfort. And what wise eloquence.
I've nothing more to say. I'll manage without it. 30

Dont vient ce mal? – Il vient de mon maleur,
Quant Saturne me feist mon fardelet
Ces maulx y meist je le croy. – *C'est foleur,*
Son seigneur es et te tiens son varlet,
Voy que Salmon escript en son rolet,
"Homme sage, ce dit il, a puissance
Sur planetes et sur leur influence." –
Je n'en croy riens, tel qu'ilz m'ont fait seray. –
Que dis tu? – Dea! certes, c'est ma creance. –
Plus ne t'en dis. – Et je m'en passeray.

Veulx tu vivre? – Dieu m'en doint la puissance! –
Il te fault . . . – Quoy? – *Remors de conscience,*
Lire sans fin. – En quoy lire? – *En science,*
Laisser les folz. – Bien j'y adviseray. –
Or le retien. – J'en ay bien souvenance. –
N'atens pas tant que tourne a desplaisance,
Plus ne t'en dis. – Et je m'en passeray.

PROBLEME

Fortune fus par clers jadis nommee
Que toy, Françoys, crie et nomme murtriere
Qui n'es homme d'aucune renommee,
Meilleur que toy fais user en plastriere
Par povreté et fouÿer en carriere,
S'a honte vis te dois tu doncques plaindre?
Tu n'es pas seul si ne te dois complaindre,
Regarde et voy de mes fais de jadis,
Mains vaillans homs par moy mors et roidis
Et n'es, ce sçais, envers eulx ung souillon,
Appaise toy et mets fin en tes dis,
Par mon conseil prens tout en gré, Villon.

Where do your troubles come from? From bad luck,
When Saturn packed my bags for me
I guess he slipped in these woes. *That's insane.*
You're his lord and you act like his slave.
Look what Solomon wrote in his book, 35
"A wise man," he says, "has authority
Over the planets and their influence."
I don't believe it, as they made me I'll be.
What are you saying? Just so, that's what I believe.
I've nothing more to say. I'll manage without it. 40

You want to live? God give me the strength.
You need . . . What? *To feel penitent,*
Read endlessly. Read in what? *Philosophy,*
And shun fools. I'll take your advice.
Then remember it. I have it fixed in mind. 45
Don't wait until you turn from bad to worse.
I've nothing more to say. I'll manage without it.

PROBLEM

Fortune I was named by scholars long ago
Whom you, François, insult and call murderer,
You a man without any fame at all,
Better men than you I've broken by plaster-making,
By poverty and digging rocks in quarries,
Must you whimper just because you live in shame? 6
You're not the only one so don't complain,
Stop and reflect on my deeds of old,
Through me many brave men are dead and stiff,
And as you know, next to them you're a scullion,
Shut up and stop making a fuss,
I suggest you take things as they come, Villon. 12

Contre grans roys me suis bien anymee
Le temps qui est passé ça en arriere,
Priam occis et toute son armee,
Ne luy valut tour, donjon, ne barriere,

Et Hannibal demoura il derriere?
En Cartaige par Mort le feis attaindre,
Et Scypion l'Affriquan feis estaindre,
Julles Cesar au Senat je vendis,
En Egipte Pompee je perdis,
En mer noyé Jason en ung bouillon
Et une fois Romme et Rommains ardis,
Par mon conseil prens tout en gré, Villon.

Alixandre qui tant feist de hemee,
Qui voulut veoir l'estoille pouciniere
Sa personne par moy fut envlimee,
Alphasar roy en champ sur sa baniere
Rué jus mort, cela est ma maniere,
Ainsi l'ay fait, ainsi le maintendray,
Autre cause ne raison n'en rendray,
Holofernes l'ydolastre mauldis
Qu'occist Judith et dormoit entandis
De son poignart dedens son pavillon.
Absalon, quoy? en fuyant le pendis,
Par mon conseil prens tout en gré, Villon.

Pour ce, Françoys, escoute que te dis,
Se riens peusse sans Dieu de Paradis
A toy n'autre ne demourroit haillon
Car, pour ung mal, lors j'en feroye dix,
Par mon conseil prens tout en gré, Villon.

QUATRAIN

Je suis Françoys dont il me poise,
Né de Paris emprès Pontoise
Et de la corde d'une toise
Sçaura mon col que mon cul poise.

VILLON'S EPITAPH

Brother humans who after us live on
Do not make your hearts hard against us
For if you show pity to wretches like us
God will the sooner show mercy to you,
You see us, five or six, hanging here, *5*
As for the flesh we pampered too much
A little while ago it was eaten and rotted away
And we the bones turn into ashes and dust,
Let no one make jokes at our fate
But pray God that He will absolve us all. *10*

Because we call you "brothers" there's no need
To be angry, though we were put to death
By justice: anyway, you understand
Not everyone is born with good sense,
Make our excuses, now we've passed on *15*
Before the Son of the Virgin Mary
That His mercy shall not, for us, go dry
Which keeps us from the thunderbolts of hell,
We are dead, let no one harass us
But pray God that He will absolve us all. *20*

The rain has rinsed and washed us
And the sun has dried us and blackened us,
Magpies and ravens have caved our eyes
And plucked out our beards and eyebrows,
Never, at no time, can we stay still, *25*
Now here, now there, as the wind shifts
At its whim without end it carries us
Pocked by birds worse than a sewing thimble,
Therefore don't be one of our brotherhood
But pray God that He will absolve us all. *30*

Prince Jesus, master over all,
Don't let us fall in the clutches of Hell,
We've no accounts to settle down there,
Humans, there's nothing in this to laugh about,
But pray God that He will absolve us all. *35*

LOUENGE A LA COURT

Tous mes cinq sens, yeulx, oreilles et bouche,
Le nez, et vous, le sensitif aussi,
Tous mes membres ou il y a reprouche,
En son endroit ung chascun die ainsi,
"Souvraine Court par qui sommes icy
Vous nous avez gardé de desconfire,
Or la langue seule ne peut souffire
A vous rendre souffisantes louenges
Si parlons tous, fille du souvrain Sire,
Mere des bons et seur des benois anges."

Cuer, fendez vous ou percez d'une broche
Et ne soyez au moins plus endurcy
Qu'au desert fut la forte bise roche
Dont le peuple des Juifs fut adoulcy,
Fondez lermes et venez a mercy
Comme humble cuer qui tendrement souspire,
Louez la Court, conjointe au Saint Empire,
L'eur des Françoys, le confort des estranges,
Procreee lassus ou ciel empire,
Mere des bons et seur des benois anges.

Et vous mes dens, chascune si s'esloche,
Saillez avant, rendez toutes mercy
Plus hautement qu'orgue, trompe, ne cloche
Et de maschier n'ayez ores soussy,
Considerez que je feusse transsy,
Foye, pommon et rate qui respire
Et vous, mon corps, qui vil estes et pire
Qu'ours ne pourceau qui fait son nyt es fanges,
Louez la Court, avant qu'il vous empire,
Mere des bons et seur des benois anges.

Prince, trois jours ne vueillez m'escondire
Pour moy pourveoir et aux miens "a Dieu" dire,
Sans eulx argent je n'ay, icy n'aux changes,
Court tiumphant, *fiat,* sans me desdire,
Mere des bons et seur des benois anges.

PRAISE TO THE COURT

All my five senses, eyes, ears, and mouth,
Nose, and you as well, my sense of touch,
All my members which suffer reproach,
Each at its station speaks as follows,
"Sovereign Court by whom we are here 5
You have preserved us from perishing
And since the tongue alone isn't enough
To render you sufficient praise
We all speak, daughter of the sovereign Lord,
Mother of the good and sister of the blessed angels." 10

Break, heart, or be transpierced
And do not be at least any harder
Than the hard gray rock in the desert
By which the Jews were given water,
Weep your tears and come in thanks 15
As a humble heart tenderly sighing,
Extol the Court, one with the Holy Empire,
Joy of the French, safety of foreigners,
Created in the empire of the skies,
Mother of the good and sister of the blessed angels. 20

And you my teeth, each come loose,
Jump forward and all give thanks
Louder than an organ, trumpet, or bell
And don't worry at present about chewing,
Bear in mind I would be dead now, 25
Liver, lungs, and spleen which still breathe
And you, my body, which is vile and worse
Than a bear or pig who beds in his excrement,
Praise the Court, before your lot gets worse,
Mother of the good and sister of the blessed angels. 30

Prince, would you begrudge me three days
To get ready and tell my family farewell,
But for them I've no money, here or at the changer's,
Triumphant Court, *fiat,* without refusing me,
Mother of the good and sister of the blessed angels. 35

QUESTION AU CLERC DU GUICHET

Que vous semble de mon appel
Garnier? Feis je sens ou folie?
Toute beste garde sa pel,
Qui la contraint, efforce ou lie,
S'elle peult elle se deslie,
Quant donc par plaisir voluntaire
Chantee me fut ceste omelie
Estoit il lors temps de moy taire?

Se feusse des hoirs Hue Cappel
Qui fut extrait de boucherie
On ne m'eust parmy ce drappel
Fait boire en ceste escorcherie,
Vous entendez bien joncherie?
Mais quant ceste paine arbitraire
On me jugea par tricherie
Estoit il lors temps de moy taire?

Cuidiez vous que soubz mon cappel
N'ëust tant de philosophie
Comme de dire, "J'en appel"?
Si avoit, je vous certiffie,
Combien que point trop ne m'y fie,
Quant on me dist, present notaire,
"Pendu serez!" je vous affie,
Estoit il lors temps de moy taire?

Prince, se j'eusse eu la pepie
Pieça je feusse ou est Clotaire
Aux champs debout comme une espie,
Estoit il lors temps de moy taire?

QUESTION TO THE GATE KEEPER

What do you think of my appeal,
Garnier? Does it make sense or not?
Every animal saves its skin,
If someone traps, beats or captures it, *4*
It runs away if it can,
When, therefore, in willful caprice
They sang me that homily,
Was it then time to hold my tongue? *8*

If I were an heir of Hue Cappel
Descended from the butchery
They wouldn't have, through cloth,
Made me drink in that tannery, *12*
Can you see through my euphemisms?
But when this arbitrary sentence
Was treacherously handed down
Was it then time to hold my tongue? *16*

Do you think that under my hat
There wasn't enough philosophy
As to blurt out, "I appeal"?
There was, I can assure you, *20*
Although I know it does no good,
When they told me, before the notary,
"You shall be hanged!" I swear,
Was it then time to hold my tongue? *24*

Prince, if I had caught the pip
Long ago I'd have been where Clotaire is
Standing high over a field like a lookout,
Was it then time to hold my tongue? *28*

NOTES

Short of a full textual commentary, there is very little help that notes to Villon can give. Not being prepared myself to provide such a commentary, I have avoided all pretense at explication and have kept the notes to a bare minimum.

THE LEGACY

6 *Vegetius:* a fourth-century Roman writer, author of *Epitoma rei militaris.*

16 *was wont:* this is the only word we have for *souloir,* and perhaps the archaism is not out of place in this part of the poem.

18 *Envisaging her:* David Kuhn raises the possibility that this is a play on the locution, *voyant le peuple,* "in view of the people," as applied to public executions, and that the line should be translated, "With her as witness, and me looking on."

52 *winds on her spindle: Cf. Twelfth Night,* Act I, Scene III: "It hangs like flax on a distaff, and I hope to see a housewife take thee between her legs, and spin it off."

70 *Guillaume Villon:* Villon's foster-father, chaplain of Saint-Benoît-le-Bétourné. *Cf. Testament,* 850.

72 *my tents and my pavilion:* trappings of knighthood.

81 *Ythier Marchant:* of a rich Parisian family. *Cf. Testament,* 970, 1024.

84 *Jean le Cornu:* of a family of financiers; became criminal clerk to the Châtelet. *Cf. Testament,* 990.

89 *Saint Amant:* Clerk of the Treasury. *Cf. Testament,* 1007.

90 *The White Horse:* a tavern sign. The signs were shaped like the animals, and students would remove them and set them coupling.

91 *Blarru:* a goldsmith.

93 *decree:* issued in 1215, the decree, *Omnis utriusque sexus,* ("All of one sex or the other . . .") ordered all Christians to confess to the parish priest at least once a year. In 1409 the Mendicant friars also obtained the right of hearing confession, a right reaffirmed by the "Carmelite" bull of 1449.

97 *Robert Valée:* a young man from a rich family of financiers.

102 *Trumillières:* a tavern.

111 *Maupensé:* perhaps Paul de mal Pencé, a figure in the fifteenth-century farce *La Reformeresse,* a kind of Simple Simon or Tom Fool.

112 *Art of Memory:* the *Ars memorativa,* a popular inspirational work of the time.

120 *Saint-Jacques:* the church Saint-Jacques-de-la-Boucherie.

123 *Jacques Cardon:* a clothing merchant. *Cf. Testament,* 1776.

130 *Regnier de Montigny:* born of a noble family, he was one of the "Coquillards." Having been hanged in 1457 he does not figure in *The Testament.*

131 *Jean Raguier: Cf. Testament,* 1070.

137 *lord of Grigny:* Philippe Brunel, a quarrelsome nobleman. *Cf. Testament,* 1346, 1941. The castle of Nijon was already in ruins.

145 *Jacques Raguier: Cf. Testament,* 1038.

146 *Popin waterhole:* a watering trough on the Right Bank.

151 *Jacobin:* name given the Dominican monks who lived on the Rue Saint-Jacques in Paris.

153 *Jean Mautaint:* Examiner at the Châtelet. *Cf. Testament,* 1366.

154 *Pierre Basanier:* notary at the Châtelet. *Cf. Testament,* 1362.

155 *the lord:* Robert d'Estouteville, Provost of Paris. *Cf. Testament,* 1369.

157 *Fournier: Cf. Testament,* 1030.

166 *The guy toting her off: The Cow* was located on the Rue Troussevache, "Tote-the-Cow Street."

175 *"The Three Lilies":* perhaps one of the rooms in the Châtelet prison, and a play on *lits,* "beds."

177 *Perrenet Marchant:* bailiff at the Châtelet. The "Bar" would be the so-called Bar Sinister of bastards. *Cf. Testament,* 764, 937, 1094.

185 *Loup and Cholet: Cf. Testament,* 1102, 1110, 1113.

201–2 *Colin Laurens, Girard Gossouyn, Jean Marceau:* old, rich merchants of Paris. *Cf. Testament,* 1275.

206 *blancs:* small coins.

207 *They'll have eaten many a meal: Ilz mangeront maint bon morceau* is thought to be the equivalent of, "They'll eat dandelions by the roots."

209 *nomination:* a letter of eligibility for a benefice.

217 *Guillaume Cotin, Thibault de Victry:* old, rich canons of Notre-Dame. *Cf. Testament,* 1306.

223 *Guillaume Gueuldry's hostel:* a house owned by Notre-Dame and rented to a butcher who never paid his rent. *Cf. Testament,* 1313.

229 *pigeons:* slang for "prisoners."

249 *Mendicants:* friars consisting of the Jacobins, the Franciscans, the Carmelites, and the Augustinians.
250 *Daughters of God, Beguines:* nuns.
253 *Fifteen Signs:* signs of the end of the world.
258 *Jean de la Garde: Cf. Testament,* 1354, 1919.
259 *Saint-Maur:* Saint-Maur-les-Fossés, where cripples went for miraculous cures.
263 *Saint Anthony:* St. Anthony's Fire was a disease, apparently one involving burning fevers. *Cf. Testament,* 600.
265 *Mereboeuf: Cf. Testament,* 1046.
266 *Nicolas de Louvieux: Cf. Testament,* 1047.
272 *Prince:* the Prince of Fools, who gave away cardboard coins at the carnival.
278 *Salvation:* the Angelus.
281ff See A. Burger, "L'Entroubli de Villon *(Lais,* XXXVXL)," *Romania,* 79 (1958), pp. 485–95.
315 *Who doesn't eat, shit, or piss:* This may be only the secondary meaning; the traditional interpretation, "Who doesn't eat figs or dates," may actually be primary. (David Kuhn)

THE TESTAMENT

6 *Thibault d'Aussigny:* Bishop of Orléans, who imprisoned Villon at Meung.
34 *Cotart:* the prayer for Cotart's soul begins on line 1230.
37 *Picard style:* the Picards were a heretical sect that did not believe in prayer. Their headquarters were at Douai and Lille.
48 *psalm Deus laudem:* Psalm 108, 8th verse (Douay): "May the days of his life be few and his bishopric pass to another." See N. Edelman, "A Scriptural Key to Villon's Testament," in *Modern Language Notes,* 72 (1957), pp. 345–51.
56 *Louis:* Louis XI, who had become king in 1461.
87 *until he dies:* this could as easily be translated "until it dies," referring to "heart."
101 *a fair city:* the City of God.
113–4 *Roman de la Rose:* the allegorical romance begun by Guillaume de Lorris and continued by Jean de Meung. The passage Villon has in mind comes, however, from the *Testament* by Jean de Meung. Perhaps Villon saw a manuscript in which it preceded the *Roman* and appeared to be a kind of introduction, or "very beginning."
130ff *Diomedes:* this story is told, among other places, in Augustine's *City of God.*
157 *maligned:* we might expect the phrase to read, "he never harmed/ Anyone again," but all the manu-

scripts agree on *mesdit*. See H. Sten, "Pour l'interpretation de Villon," in *Romania*, 71 (1950), pp. 509–12.

159 *Valerian:* Valère-Maxim.

211 *Rejoice:* Ecclesiastes, 11: 9.

214 *Childhood:* Ecclesiastes, 11: 10 (King James).

217 *My days: Job,* 7: 6.

264 *What I have written: John,* 19: 22 (King James).

265 *Let's leave the church where it lies: Laissons le moustier ou il est* was an expression meaning, "Let's change the subject," in this case literally applicable.

285 *Jacques Coeur:* one of the richest men of France, who died November 25, 1456.

292 Psalm 103, verses 15 and 16 (King James).

309–11 *folded-back collars, coverchief, caul:* modes of dress which were signs of a woman's station in life.

330 *Flora:* a Roman courtesan.

331 *Archipiada:* Alcibiades, who was taken to be a woman in the Middle Ages.

331 *Thaïs:* mistress of Alexander the Great.

341 *the queen:* Jeanne de Navarre, a queen of France who according to the story romanced with students and then had them thrown out the window into the Seine.

345 *The queen:* perhaps Queen Blanche of Bourgogne, wife of Charles IV, condemned for adultery.

347 *Big-footed Bertha, Beatrice, Alice:* according to L. Thuasne, heroines of a medieval *chanson de geste, Hervi de Metz.* Bertha is the niece of Beatrice, who is the daughter-in-law of Alice.

357ff *And where's the third Callixtus:* except for those cited in the *envoi,* all the characters in the *ballade* were contemporary and died between 1456 and 1461.

385ff *For be it His Holiness the Pope:* the *ballade* is written in Old French and contains many grammatical errors, surely deliberate.

448 See H. Sten, "Pour l'interpretation de Villon," *Romania,* 71 (1950), pp. 509–12.

553–5 See J. Rychner, "Pour le Testament de Villon (vers 553–5 et 685)," *Romania,* 74 (1953), pp. 383–9.

565 *Fremin:* doubtless an imaginary secretary.

600 *Saint Anthony's Fire:* a disease. *Cf. Legacy,* 263.

601 *decree:* "It is more tolerable if the fault is kept hidden and if the practice is widespread."

732 *Jeanneton:* a name for any girl at all.

737 *Tacque Thibault:* one of the Duke of Berry's men, universally hated in the fourteenth century. Villon applies his name insultingly to Thibault d'Aussigny.

738 *cold water:* a reference to the water torture, where the subject was forced to drink quantities of water through a cloth.

750 *Master Robert:* possibly Master Robert Valée of *Legacy,* 97.

752 *Lombard:* usurer. For another interpretation, see J. Frappier, "Pour le commentaire de Villon, Testament, vers 751–2," *Romania,* 80 (1959), pp. 191–207.

764 *Bastard of the Bar:* Perrenet Marchand. Cf. *Legacy,* 177, and *Testament,* 937 and 1094.

774 *Moreau, Provins, Robin Turgis:* a meat-roaster, a pastry-maker, and the proprietor of *The Pine Cone.*

797 *Who saved:* the doctrine of the Redemption.

813 *Jesus' parable: Luke* 16: 19–31 (King James).

838 *nine high Orders:* the nine choirs of Angels.

850 *Guillaume de Villon:* Villon's foster-father. *Cf. Legacy,* 70.

858 *"The Tale of the Devil's Fart":* presumably a lost early work by Villon.

859 *Guy Tabary:* being questioned by the police after the robbery of the College of Navarre, Tabary told the whole story very truthfully.

885 *Egyptian woman:* Saint Mary of Egypt.

886 *Theophilus:* hero of a thirteenth-century play by Rutebeuf, *Le Miracle de Theophile,* who made a pact with the devil in order to keep his job.

910 See E. Vidal "Deux legs de Villon," in *Romance Philology,* Vol. XII (1958–59), pp. 251–57.

911 *heart or liver:* a play on *cuer* as sentiments and as the physical heart, and on *foi,* "faith," and *foie,* "liver."

917 *écu, targe:* coins; also shields.

922 *Michault:* a legendary figure known for his sexual prowess. *Cf. Testament,* 1338.

937 *Perrenet of the Bar:* Perrenet Marchand. *Cf. Legacy,* 177, and *Testament,* 764 and 1094.

939 *my damsel:* See H. Sten, "Pour l'interprétation de Villon," *Romania,* 71 (1950), pp. 509–12.

942ff *False beauty who makes me pay so dear:* the French text of this *ballade* has an acrostic, "François," in the first stanza, and another, "Martha," in the second. The "Rose" of line 910 may be just a pet name.

954 *Help me, help me, both the bigger and smaller!:* a play on the expression, *"Crier le grant Haro";* there was no *mineur* Haro. (David Kuhn)

970 *Ythier Marchant: Cf. Legacy,* 81, and *Testament,* 1024.

990 *Jean Cornu: Cf. Legacy,* 84.

995 *Pierre Bobignon:* advocate at the Châtelet.

1007 *Pierre Saint-Amant: Cf. Legacy,* 89.

1014–5 *Denis Hesselin:* a fiscal judge.

1017 *Turgis:* proprietor of *The Pine Cone. Cf. Testament* 774, 1054.
1029 *Templars:* Knights Templar.
1030 *Fournier: Cf. Legacy,* 157.
1038–9 *Jacques Raguier: Cf. Legacy,* 145.
1039 *Grève:* Place de Grève, in Paris.
1046 *Merebeuf, Nicolas de Louviers: Cf. Legacy,* 265.
1053 *Machecoue's:* a poultry shop.
1054 *Robin Turgis: Cf. Testament* 774, 1017.
1060 See M. Dubois, "Poitou et Poitevins (De Benoît à Villon)," in *Romania,* 80 (1959), pp. 243–53.
1070 *Jean Raguier: Cf. Legacy,* 131.
1071 *the Twelve:* the mounted guard of the Provost of Paris.
1073 *tallemousse:* a three-cornered, conical pastry.
1075 *Bailly's:* the house of Jean de Bailly, a functionary.
1076 *Maubué:* a water fountain.
1078 *Prince of Fools:* head of the brotherhood of fools, or persons who played the clown in various festivities. *Cf. Legacy,* 272.
1086 *Two-twenty:* the municipal police.
1094 *Perrenet: Cf. Legacy,* 177, and *Testament,* 764, 937.
1102 *Cholet: Cf. Legacy,* 185, and *Testament,* 1113.
1110 *Jean le Lou: Cf. Legacy,* 185.
1118 *The Woodworker:* the nickname of Jean Mahé, sergeant at the Châtelet.
1126 *Jean Riou:* Captain of Archers of the city of Paris.
1142 *Robinet Trascaille:* tax collector at Château-Thierry.
1157 *Abbess of Pourras:* Huguette de Hamel, who was removed from her post in 1463 for immorality.
1159 *Devotes, Beguines:* orders of nuns.
1161 *Turlupins:* heretics.
1174 *Jean de Poullieu:* Jean de Poliaco, a Doctor of the University of Paris.
1178 *Jean de Meung:* one of the authors of the *Roman de la Rose.*
1179 *Matheolus:* author of *Liber lamentationum.*
1210 *Macée:* a judge, insultingly called "she."
1214-21 See D. Legge, "On Villon's *Testament* CXXIII," in *Modern Language Review,* Vol. 44 (1949), pp. 199–206.
1222 *Jean Laurens:* spice merchant and speculator in salt.
1230 *Jean Cotart: Cf. Testament,* 34.
1232 *patart:* a coin of very small worth.
1238 *Father Noah: Genesis,* 9: 20.
1239 *Lot: Genesis,* 19: 30–36.
1243 *Architriclinus:* the name given to the ruler of the feast, *John* 2: 9.
1271 *écus, targes: Cf. Testament,* 917.
1275 *three poor little orphans: Cf. Legacy,* 201–2.

NOTES

1283 *Pierre Richier:* headmaster of a school.
1284 *Donatus:* the standard Latin grammar text of the Middle Ages.
1287 *Ave salus, tibi decus:* a parody of a hymn to the Virgin in which these verses appear:
Ave, decus virginum,
Ave, salus hominum.
Saluts, like *écus,* were gold coins.
1292 *great Credo:* apparently this was a facetious expression meaning long-term credit.
1294 *I rip my long tabard:* a reference to Saint Martin, who tore his cloak and gave half to the beggar.
1306 *poor little clerks: Cf. Legacy,* 217.
1313 *the house of Guillaume Gueuldry:* a butcher shop whose owner was always behind in rent.
1322 *Eighteen Clerks:* the *Collège des Dix-Huits Clercs.*
1338 *Michault Culdoe:* Thuasne remarks that Culdoe's name was actually Michel: "But in the courtly phraseology of the period, 'Michault' had a special meaning which our legatee was, it seems, impotent to justify." *Cf. Testament,* 922.
1339 *Charlot Taranne:* a rich Parisian.
1346 *lord of Grigny: Cf. Legacy,* 137.
1354 *Thibault de la Garde: Cf. Legacy,* 258, and *Testament,* 1919. "Thibaud" and "Jean" were both synonyms for cuckold.
1360 *Genevois:* solicitor at the Châtelet.
1362 *Basanier: Cf. Legacy,* 154.
1366 *Mautaint, Rosnel:* examiners at the Châtelet. *Cf. Legacy,* 153.
1378ff *At daybreak when the sparrow-hawk disports:* this *ballade,* written for Robert d'Estouteville (*Cf. Legacy,* 155), has the name of his wife, Ambroise de Lore, as acrostic.
1406 *Jean Perdrier:* concierge of the royal castle at Loges.
1414 *Taillevent:* the *Viandier Taillevent,* a cookbook.
1418 *Macquaire:* thought by some to be a celebrated bad cook of the time, by others to be Saint Macquire of Alexandria, who had power over devils.
1457 *André Courault:* solicitor in Parliament.
1458 *Gontier:* protagonist of a poem by Philippe de Vitry, *"Le Dit Franc Gontier,"* which praised the simple joys of country life.
1508 *damsel of Bruyères:* the proprietress of the hotel, *Le Pet au Diable,* "The Devil's Fart."
1548 *Macrobius:* fifth-century Roman philosopher.
1551 *Montmartre:* a nunnery situated on Montmartre.
1554 *Mount Valerian:* a hermitage.
1628–9 *Marion the Idol, Big Jeanne:* madams of brothels.

NOTES

1663 *Marion the Idol's: Cf. Testament,* 1628.

1671–2 *travel to Montpipeau/Or Rueil:* locutions meaning "to steal" and "to rob."

1675 *Colin de Cayeux:* took part along with Villon and Guy Tabary in the College of Navarre robbery. He was finally caught and put to death.

1728 *Fifteen Score:* the *Hôpital des Quinze-Vingts,* a home for the blind located in the Cemetery of the Innocents.

1776 *Jacquet Cardon: Cf. Legacy,* 123.

1779 *bergeronnette:* a shepherd's ditty.

1780, 82 *"Marionette," "Open Your Door Guillemette";* popular songs.

1796 *Lomer:* perhaps a Pierre Lomer who in 1456 had been given the job of getting prostitutes off the streets of the Cité.

1803 *Ogier the Dane:* the hero of *La Chevalierie Ogier de Danemarche* by Raimbert de Paris.

1805 *Alain Chartier's legacy:* in *La belle dame sans merci* he wrote:

> I leave to the sick-with-love
> Who have hopes of being cured
> To compose songs, speeches and poems
> Each according to his understanding

1812 *Jacques James: Cf. Testament,* 1944.

1828 *Captain of the Watch: Cf. Legacy,* 169.

1845 *Jean de Calais:* notary at the Châtelet in charge of verifying wills.

1868 *Sainte-Avoye:* an Augustinian convent in Paris, the chapel of which was on the second floor.

1892–93 *Rest eternal grant him,* etc.: *Cf.* the Mass of the Dead: *Requiem aeternam dona eis, Domine, et lux perpetua, luceat eis.*

1905 *the big bell:* perhaps *La Jacqueline,* a large, fragile bell in Notre-Dame.

1919 *Jean de la Garde: Cf. Legacy,* 258 and *Testament,* 1354.

1941 *Philippe Brunel: Cf. Legacy,* 137 and *Testament,* 1346.

1943 *Jacques Raguier: Cf. Legacy,* 145 and *Testament,* 1038.

1944 *Jacques James: Cf. Testament,* 1812.

MISCELLANEOUS POEMS

VI. *Ballade:* "I die of thirst beside the fountain." This poem appears to have been written in a competition held by Charles d'Orléans, in which the host provided the first line and each of the guests went on from there. Fifteen poems have come down to us with the same first line as this *ballade*.

VII. *Epistle to Marie d'Orléans.* Marie d'Orléans, born in 1457, was the daughter of the Duke of Orléans. The epigraph is from Virgil's fourth *Eclogue,* line 7: "Now a new progeny comes down from heaven on high."

42–3 *Delectasti me . . . :* "For thou, Lord, hast made me glad through thy work." Psalm 92:4

50–1 *Inimicum putes . . . :* "Consider as an enemy him who will praise you to your face." Cato, *Disticha de moribus.*

108 *Patrem . . . :* "The child follows the father."

118–20 *Nova . . . :* a variant of the epigraph.

IX. *Request to Monsieur de Bourbon.*

27 *cross:* on one side of coins there was a cross.

X. *The Debate Between Villon's Body and Heart.* For a discussion of this poem, see L. F. Benedetto, "Il dialogo di Villon col suo Cuore," *Atti della Accademia delle Scienze di Torino,* Vol. LXXXVII (1952–53).

XV. *Question to the Gate Keeper.*

2 *Garnier:* Etienne Garnier was gate keeper of the Châtelet prison.

CHRONOLOGY

1431 François Montcorbier, or François des Loges, later to become known as François Villon after his guardian and benefactor, Guillaume de Villon, chaplain of Saint-Benoît-le-Bétourné, was born in Paris.

1449 He received his *baccalauréat* from the University of Paris.

1451 He probably took part in a student prank which involved removing a stone landmark, the Pet-au-Diable (The Devil's Fart), from in front of the house of a Mademoiselle de Bruyères. Villon mentions having written *The Tale of the Devil's Fart,* which, if it really existed, is lost.

1452 He received his *licence* and *maître és arts* from the University of Paris.

1455 In the Cloister of Saint-Benoît Villon was drawn into a fight with a priest and killed him. The details of the fight are given by an eyewitness—a friend of Villon's —who maintained that Villon acted in self-defense.

1456 He was pardoned for the murder. In December he apparently took part in the theft of five hundred gold *écus* from the College of Navarre, along with Guy Tabary, Dom Nicholas, Colin de Cayeux, and Petit Jean. In this same year he wrote *The Legacy*.

1457 Guy Tabary confessed to the robbery and named his accomplices, making Villon a wanted man.

1461 If we can interpret *The Testament* biographically, Villon passed the summer in the prison at Meung-sur-Loire, in the prison of the Bishop of Orléans. In October Louis XI, who was passing through the city, would have set him free. In this year he wrote *The Testament*.

1462 He was imprisoned in the Châtelet on a charge of theft, but was released a few days later on signing a pledge to return 120 *écus* to the College of Navarre.

1463 There was a fight on the Rue de la Parcheminerie, and though Villon, it appears, was only an on-looker, he was arrested and sentenced to be hanged. The sentence was set aside by an act of Parliament, but "in view of the bad way of life of the said Villon," he was sentenced to banishment from Paris for ten years.

Except for two probably apocryphal stories told by Rabelais—one in which Villon visits England, one in which he spends his last days at Saint-Maizent in Poitou—Villon, at the age of 32, vanishes from history.

SELECTED BIBLIOGRAPHY

TEXTS

Les Ballades de Villon, edited by P. Champion in *Les Sources de l'argot ancien* by L. Sainean. Vol. 1 (Paris, 1912), pp. 111–138.

François Villon, Oeuvres, edited by L. Thuasne, 3 vols. (Paris, 1923).

Le poesie di François Villon, edited in the *Scrittori di Francia* series by Ferdinando Neri (Torino, 1923).

François Villon, Oeuvres, edited in the *Classiques français du Moyen Age* series by A. Longnon, revised by L. Foulet (fourth edition, Paris, 1932).

The Complete Works of François Villon, translated (with a facing French text) and edited by Anthony Bonner (New York, 1960).

BIOGRAPHICAL AND CRITICAL WORKS

C. Marot, "Prologue aux lecteurs" in *Les Oeuvres de Francoys Villon de Paris, reveues et remises en leur entier* (Paris, 1533).

SELECTED BIBLIOGRAPHY

Théophile Gautier, "François Villon" in *Les Grotesques* (Paris, 1844).

W. Bijvanck, *Specimen d'un essai critique sur les oeuvres de François Villon. Le Petit Testament* (Leyden, 1882).

G. Paris, *Villon,* in *Les grands écrivains français* series (Paris, 1901).

M. Schwob, *François Villon et son temps* (Paris, 1912).

P. Champion, *François Villon, sa vie et son temps,* 2 vols. (Paris, 1913).

F. Desonay, *Villon* (Paris, 1933).

E. Pound, "Montcorbier, alias Villon" in *The Spirit of Romance* (New York, 1933).

I. Siciliano, *François Villon et les thèmes poétiques du Moyen Age* (Paris, 1934).

L. Cons, *État présent des études sur Villon* (Paris, 1936).

A. Burger, *Lexique de la langue de Villon* (Geneva-Paris, 1957).

G. A. Brunelli, *François Villon* (Milano, 1961).

TRANSLATIONS INTO ENGLISH

"Ballade des Dames," Luisa Stuart Constello, in *Specimen of the Early Poetry of France* (London, 1835).

Three *ballades* in *Poems,* Dante Gabriel Rossetti (London, 1870).

The Poems of Master François Villon of Paris, John Payne (London, 1874).

Ten *ballades* in *Poems and Ballades.* Second Series. Algernon Charles Swinburne (London, 1878).

The Poems of François Villon, Edward F. Chaney (Oxford, 1940).

The Poems of François Villon, H. B. McCaskie (London, 1946).

"Ballade to Our Lady," Harvey Shapiro, *Wake,* No. 9, 1950.

The Complete Works of François Villon, Anthony Bonner (New York, 1960).

Ballades and other selections, in *Imitations,* by Robert Lowell (New York, 1962).

"Ballade of the Ladies of Time Past," Richard Wilbur, *Poetry,* November, 1964.

INDEX OF FIRST LINES

PAGE

A Chartreux et a Celestins........................166

Aiez pitié, aiez pitié de moy........................194

Au poinct du jour, que l'esprevier s'esbat.......132

Au retour de dure prison........................156

Car ou soies porteur de bulles........................150

Car ou soit ly sains apostolles........................ 70

Combien que j'ay leu en ung dit..............190

Dame du ciel, regente terrienne........................100

Dictes moy ou, n'en quel pays........................ 66

En l'an de mon trentiesme aage........................ 46

En realgar, an arcenic rochier........................134

Faulse beauté qui tant me couste chier..........104

Fortune fus par clers jadis nommee..............202

Freres humains qui après nous vivez............206

Hommes faillis despourveuz de raison...........174

Icy se clost le testament........................168

INDEX

PAGE

Il n'est soing que quant on a fain................180
Je congnois bien mouches en let................178
Je meurs de seuf auprès de la fontaine............184
Je suis Françoys dont il me poise...............204
L'an quatre cens cinquante six................ 24
Le mien seigneur et prince redoubté............196
Mort, j'appelle de ta rigueur.................106
O louee conception..........................186
Or y pensez belle Gantiere................... 78
Pere Noé qui plantastes la vigne..............122
Pour ce amez tant que vouldrez............ 84
Qu'est ce que j'oy?–*Ce suis je.*–Qui?–*Ton cuer*..200
Que vous semble de mon appel.................210
Qui plus, ou est le tiers Calixte............... 68
Quoy qu'on tient belles langagieres.............140
Rencontré soit des bestes feu getans.............182
Repos eternel donne a cil.....................162
Se j'ayme et sers la belle de bon hait...........144
Sur mol duvet assis ung gras chanoine...........138
Tant grate chievre que mal gist................176
Tous mes cinq sens, yeulx, oreilles et bouche.....208